Chasing Julia

Sophia Renny

Publisher's Note: This is a work of fiction. Names, characters, places, and incidents are a product of the author's imagination. Locales and public names are sometimes used for atmospheric purposes. Any resemblance to actual people, living or dead, or to businesses, companies, events, institutions, or locales is completely coincidental.

Cover Art Credit: ©iStock.com
Cover design: © 2015 Sophia Renny

Chasing Julia/ Sophia Renny -- 1st ed.
ISBN-13:   978-1508552987
ISBN-10: 1508552983

DEDICATION

For all my Rhode Island friends.
You are true blue

CONTENTS

Prologue

Something was licking her foot.

Some*one* was licking her foot?

It was alive, whatever it was. But it didn't feel like a human tongue. It was a very small tongue. Very warm. Very sandpapery. Very into whatever was on the sole of her foot. That tongue was lapping at her skin at a frenzied pace, like her foot was a double scoop of Chunky Monkey that needed to be devoured before it melted under a blazing summer sun.

Maybe this was a dream.

Julia cracked one eye open. The eye that wasn't scrunched against her pillow. She winced as a ray of sunlight streaming in from the bedroom window struck her eyeball like a fiery hot dagger. She squeezed her eye shut. Tiny, sharp points of light pricked through her eyelid. They pulsed with the beat of her heart.

"Oh, God."

Her mouth was so dry that the words came out as a raspy whisper.

Her head throbbed. Her eyes throbbed. Even her hair seemed to be throbbing.

What in the world had she done?

She was lying on her stomach. The bed sheet beneath her scratched her skin. Something hard pressed uncomfortably into her rib cage, just below her breasts. She snaked one hand under her stomach and felt around. It wasn't the bed sheet that was causing discomfort.

What the hell was she wearing?

Was that a bustier?

She slid her hand lower.

She was still wearing panties. Satin, by the feel of them and not very substantial. Okay, that was definitely a thong. Her butt cheeks were bare.

Why was she wearing a thong? She hadn't worn those since she'd turned thirty; hipsters were more her style.

And what the *hell* was licking her foot?

Her feet were uncovered; one foot was hanging over the side of the bed. She jerked that foot inward and kicked the other foot out, connecting with what felt like a ball of fur.

"*Yip!*"

Four paws pounced on her lower back, nails digging through the bedspread.

"What the—"

"Looks like Max wants to play."

The weight of whatever creature that had tackled her was lifted away.

Julia's eyes flew open.

That was a male voice. A very recognizable male voice. Warm and deep with a little bit of gravel. Bourbon on the rocks. It poured over her skin and flowed through her veins, igniting fires deep in her belly.

But she'd never heard that voice right next to her in bed before.

This wasn't her bed.

Her eyes tracked anxiously around the room.

This was a hotel room.

The window curtains were open. In the distance she glimpsed what appeared to be the Eiffel Tower.

How did she get to Paris?

Her heart thundered in her ears as fuzzy memories infiltrated her alcohol-soaked brain.

This wasn't Paris.

This was Las Vegas.

Oh, oh, God. *What* had she done?

Slowly, painfully, she flipped over to her side to face the man lying on his side inches away from her.

Her wide eyes landed on his naked torso, followed the dark hairs of his happy trail down to where it disappeared beneath the bedcovers. He was lean, sleek and muscular; his olive-toned skin had a healthy glow. He was using one arm to prop up his head; the other held a wriggling, motley-furred, grinning little dog tucked against his chest.

She slowly lifted her eyes to his face.

His teeth flashed white; his cheeks dimpled. His toffee-colored eyes sparkled.

"Good afternoon, wife," he said. "Sleep well?"

Chapter One

Six weeks earlier

"This is a mistake. You're just going to torture yourself watching this."

Julia gave her best friend, Hannah, a belligerent look. "I *have* to watch it. It'll eat me up inside if I don't. I need to see how it was when they first met. This will help with closure."

"Okay. But don't tell me later that I didn't warn you. Do you want vodka now? Or later?"

"Both."

"Chunky Monkey now? Or later?"

"Now."

"As your best friend I confess I do feel guilty for aiding and abetting your ten pound weight gain. Promise me you'll start a diet with me tomorrow? I can't find anything in my closet that fits right anymore. I've been wearing yoga pants for the last week. Sam is starting to get a little concerned."

Julia cracked a smile. "Promise." She gave Hannah a hug that she'd intended to be quick, but it ended up lasting much longer. She shared several deep, restorative breaths with her friend before pulling away. "In case I haven't said it enough already, thanks for being there for me, Han. Love you."

Hannah beamed her signature, quirky smile. "Love you back, babe. Just hope you never have to return the favor."

"Not going to happen. Sam is true blue."

Hannah retrieved two empty bowls from Julia's kitchen cupboard. "It's good to hear you mention his name. It's been hard for me to talk about my fiancé much considering…"

"I know. I'm sorry."

"Don't be," Hannah said as she doled out generous scoops of ice cream in each bowl. "You have absolutely nothing to be sorry for. It's Joe who should be sorry."

Julia leaned against the kitchen counter. She sighed heavily. "He *was* sorry, Han. He said over and over how sorry he was. He was honest and sincere, just like he's always been. He said he had never wanted to hurt me." Her voice cracked a little.

"But he did. So, when do you think you'll be able to talk to him again?"

"I don't know."

"It's been four months. When was the last time he called?"

"Just yesterday, actually. I forgot to tell you."

"What did he say this time?"

"He just asked me to call him. That's all."

"Maybe he's worried about you watching the show tonight."

"Maybe."

Hannah slid the bowls of ice cream across the counter toward Julia. "Go get cozy. I'll grab the shot glasses."

Julia went into the living room and sat down on

the brown leather sofa facing a flat screen television affixed to the opposite wall. She set the bowls on the knotty pine coffee table.

Over the last four months, she'd spent more time in this room than any other. It was still difficult being in the bedroom, even though she'd purchased a new mattress and changed the décor. Too many memories still lingered in that space. More often than not, she ended up sleeping on the couch. It was wide, firm and comfortable.

It was a gorgeous, warm early-September evening, but she still drew a fleece-lined throw across her lap. It had become a kind of security blanket.

Hannah entered the room and set a bottle of vodka and two shot glasses on the coffee table. She plopped down on the couch close to Julia, grabbed a corner of the throw and tugged it across her legs. She gave Julia a shoulder bump. "You ready?"

"Ready as I'll ever be."

Hannah reached for the remote and turned the television on.

It was already set on the HOME channel. That had always been Julia's favorite channel, even before Tony and Joe's show had come to be.

She ate some ice cream, one eye on the commercials leading up to the show.

Rossetti & Rossetti—bold, burgundy letters on a cloudy gray background—appeared on the screen. A male announcer's voice filled Julia's living room.

"Today on Rossetti and Rossetti, the brothers will journey to the village of Conimicut, Rhode Island where a young woman has recently inherited a cottage in need of a major overhaul."

Exterior shots of a two-story 1920s era wood and

brick bungalow appeared on the screen. As the camera panned the surroundings and then showed images of Conimicut Point Park and Narragansett Bay, the announcer continued: "Tony and Joe are about to meet Willa for the first time to walk through her home. Willa was the lucky winner of a total home makeover sponsored by the HOME network and the Rhode Island Home Show."

A spoonful of ice cream lodged in Julia's throat as she got her first glimpse of her ex-fiancé since the awful, horrible day back in May when he'd broken their engagement after confessing to her that he'd fallen deeply and irrevocably in love with Willa Cochrane.

She swallowed down the ice cream and the huge lump of pain that had swelled up from her heart as the front door opened, framing a petite, brown-haired and beautiful young woman with wide blue eyes. Then the view switched to a shot from behind the woman's back, zooming in on a grinning Tony and an unsmiling Joe.

"Hello there," Tony said, with his usual charm and enthusiasm. "You must be Willa. I'm Tony Rossetti and this is my brother, Joe. It's great to meet you. Congratulations on winning the contest!"

Willa greeted them and asked them to come inside. Julia noticed that she didn't shake hands with either of the brothers. She appeared to be nervous, avoiding Joe's eyes as she led the men into her living room and shared the history of the house with them.

"She talks funny," Hannah commented, sounding snide.

"Don't be mean. Tony shared some of her background with me. She was a child prodigy. She has the I.Q. of a genius."

"An intellectual? One of those head in the clouds types, I bet."

"*Shh*. I can't hear what Joe's saying."

Willa had led the men into her dining room. Joe shoved aside the heavy velvet curtains, releasing a visible cloud of dust. Tony made a comment about the room looking like it hadn't been used that often.

"Do you like to entertain?" Joe asked Willa.

Julia was so distracted by the unusually gruff tone of his voice that she didn't hear Willa's reply.

"What do you do for a living?" Joe asked Willa next.

Reasonable questions from a contractor preparing to put together the ideal remodel plan for a homeowner. But Julia sensed the undercurrent beneath Joe's questions; his curiosity was more than professional.

He'd confessed to Julia that he'd felt drawn towards Willa the moment she'd opened that front door.

Julia wished now that he hadn't shared so many intimate details with her. But that's the way he'd always been with her since they were children: open, direct, honest. Except for those murky weeks prior to the break-up when he'd become increasingly distant, and she'd been too consumed with her wedding plans to realize something was very, very wrong.

Now everyone was in the master bedroom.

"Is this where you sleep?" Joe asked Willa, his voice low and intense.

"*Jesus*," Hannah murmured. "Can I please change the channel, Jules? This is just too cruel."

"No."

Now they were walking upstairs. Tony put his hand on Willa's lower back and made a teasing comment about how steep the stairs were. Julia was startled by a sharp bite of resentment. Tony had always been a flirt. This wasn't anything new. Why did it bother her?

Joe was inspecting the furniture. Then he reached up to touch the low ceiling. The camera shot was a wide angle showing both him and Willa in the same frame. Willa had her eyes glued to his chest. Julia couldn't blame her. Joe looked so masculine and strong, his tall, sleekly muscular build shown to its best advantage as he stretched his arm to the ceiling.

"This can be opened up to the beams," he said. "We could put a couple of skylights up here. We could even turn this space into one large master bedroom. Do you have children, Willa?"

"No… No, I'm not married."

"Let me ask you this, then. Do you see yourself living here for a long time? Raising a family here, maybe? Or will this be a summer home?"

"Yes," Willa answered softly. "I'd like to raise a family here. It's a good neighborhood."

The camera zoomed in for a close-up of Joe's face. His eyes seemed to glow, his gaze intent on Willa.

"*Gah*!" Hannah shrieked. "What the hell are we watching here? *The Bachelor*?" Her outburst drowned out the voiceover.

The show cut to commercials.

"Sure you want to keep watching?" Hannah asked, her worried eyes scrutinizing Julia's pale face.

Julia grimaced. "Yes. But I need a shot."

Hannah set her empty bowl on the coffee table and poured out a shot of vodka for each of them. She handed Julia a glass and tapped hers against it. "How about we do a shot for every time they zoom in on Joe's face?"

Julia tossed her head back and downed the shot in one gulp. Hot liquid poured down her throat and burned her lungs. She held out the empty glass for a refill. "Only if you're planning to crash here tonight. No way am I letting you drive home drunk."

"Fine with me," Hannah agreed as she refilled both their glasses. "I don't have anything on the agenda for tomorrow anyway. Thank God tomorrow's Friday, right?"

Hannah ran a graphic design business from her home. Julia had first met her over ten years ago when Julia had been outsourcing some print materials for an event. Hannah was the same age; they'd hit it off immediately. Hannah's bubbly personality brought out Julia's inner playful side—the impish, sometimes devilish personality that she rarely revealed to her parents, or to anyone else, now that she thought about it. Her parents had raised her to be the perfect lady; she'd always done her very best to live up to their high expectations.

She was pretty sure they were watching this episode right now, too, though they hadn't mentioned the Rossetti brothers' show once in her presence since May. Her mother had taken Julia's cue and avoided bringing Joe's name into their conversations. Diane Kelly had been just as devastated as Julia when Joe had broken the engagement—probably even more so. She had been convinced since Julia was a little girl that her daughter would marry Joe someday.

Strangely, her mother was the first person Julia had thought of when Joe had broken things off. Diane had intertwined her expectations and dreams so closely with her daughter's that Julia had only recently begun to wonder if she had been living her mother's dream all this time and not her own.

"And we're back," Hannah said in an aside as the Rossetti & Rossetti logo flashed on the screen again.

Everyone was in Willa's kitchen now. Tony was raving about the 1950s era appliances. Joe was running his hands along a built-in wall unit. They were talking about how much counter space Willa wanted in her kitchen. Joe said they'd have to take the wall unit out to have enough space for the counters. He opened one of the drawers.

Suddenly, Willa came running towards him and shouted, "No!" She reached inside the drawer and pulled something out. It looked like a child's drawing.

Julia leaned forward, her heart thumping painfully as she watched her ex-fiancé brush his fingers down Willa's arm and then clasp her wrist. He brought both of their hands upwards so he could get a closer look at the picture. The camera zoomed in on both him and Willa as she explained that she'd drawn the picture when she was seven years old.

And there it was.

Julia could practically hear the *click* as their eyes met. Something softened in both of their expressions. It was like they were the only two people in that room.

"Holy shit," Hannah breathed.

Julia was finding it extremely difficult to breathe at all.

And then Tony was moving into the shot, bursting that intimate bubble, forcing Willa and Joe's attention back to the task at hand. Tony's voice was calm, his manner confident. He took charge as he guided Willa outside to talk about landscaping and other design elements.

Joe didn't speak with Willa again for the remainder of that segment. There was a brief interview of him talking about his overall first impressions of Willa's house. He concluded by saying, "That kitchen wall unit is a well-made piece of furniture that clearly holds some special memories for Willa. I'm going to do everything I can to keep it intact in that room. But, if she wants the counter space, it'll have to come out." He shook his head, looking troubled. "I don't want her to be unhappy." And then he seemed to realize what he'd revealed with that comment. His expression went flat. "It'll be a tough choice for her, but sometimes you have to sacrifice sentimentality for the sake of practical design."

The scene switched to an interview with Willa. The drawing was on the table in front of her. "I was very surprised when I opened the front door," she said quietly. "I wasn't expecting the brothers to be so...young... They seemed very competent. Tony asked some good questions. Joe seems to like old furniture."

"It sounds like keeping that wall unit intact is important to you," the faceless interviewer opined.

"Yes. I didn't realize until that moment just how important it would be." Willa's voice was shaky. "I'm not sure how they'll be able to work around it. I'm really looking forward to seeing the designs they come up with."

Cut to commercial.

"How many times did the camera zoom in on his face since the last commercial?" Hannah asked. "I got distracted."

"Twice."

Hannah poured another shot for both of them. "Bottom's up." They each threw one shot back and then another in quick succession.

Julia swiped her hand across her mouth. She was beginning to feel slightly drunk. Maybe more than slightly. Her head was buzzing. Her heart felt numb. But her heart had felt numb since May. Nothing new there. She asked Hannah to pour another shot.

The next few scenes moved at a quicker pace. Willa and her friend Collette went to Joe and Tony's office to take a look at the designs. Julia's hearing was a little fuzzy as she watched Willa offer the guys a tin of cookies. A voiceover obscured whatever conversation was taking place as the announcer mentioned in a jovial tone that Willa had made cookies, but that she might take them back if she didn't like the designs the guys had come up with. Everyone sat down at a conference table. Then the screen split, showing the 3-D designs on one half and Willa and Collette's reactions on the other.

Hannah guffawed when Collette said "Holy Crap" on camera. "That lady's a riot."

"I've met her," Julia said, her voice sounding slurred to her own ears. "She and her friends are all the same. A little nosy and loud. But nice."

The camera was now focused on a conversation between Joe and Willa. He was promising her that he would come up with some way to keep a part of the wall unit and Willa's happy memories of her aunt in the kitchen. A close-up of his solemn face as Willa agreed to his plans faded to an interview with Willa: "It wasn't an easy decision. But Joe promised that he'd keep my aunt's memory in that room. I believe him... I can tell when someone is lying to me. Joe doesn't lie."

Except to himself, Julia thought, bitterness showing its ugly claws.

She must have spoken the words out loud. Hannah flung her arm around Julia's shoulders. "We're halfway through. You want to keep watching?"

Julia nodded her head before resting it on her friend's shoulder.

Now it was demolition day. Hannah laughed at images of the petite and plump Collette in her goggles helping Joe tear out some kitchen cabinets. And there was Willa swinging a sledgehammer at the dining room wall. She looked angry. Tony interrupted her work and asked her to come into the kitchen to see the progress Joe and Collette had made.

Julia lifted her head from Hannah's shoulder and perked up her ears. Something had changed between Joe and Willa since the meeting in the office. There was a new kind of tension in the air, so palpable Julia could almost feel it. Joe was explaining that he'd been able to keep the wall unit intact and asking if Willa would like to have it installed in her garage.

"Why?" Willa asked, her voice curt. "I don't need a cabinet in the garage."

"Storage?"

"This wood is too pretty to be in a garage. You said you'd make something out of the material."

"Yes, I did. I just wanted to check with you first."

"That's what I want. I want you to make something that will keep my aunt in this room. Like you said you would."

"And I will."

Joe's voice was gentle and patient, but his expression was impassive. It was very clear that Willa was anxious about the cabinet, and he was trying to soothe her. But there was something else there, an underlying conversation taking place. The cameras focused on the two of them just standing there looking at each other.

And then Tony stepped into the picture. "Well, it looks like we've answered that question. Let's get out of the way now and let the crew haul this outside. Willa, do you want to help me rip out the carpet in the upstairs bedrooms?"

"She looked pissed off about something," Hannah commented.

Tony's face appeared on the screen in a confession cam interview. "Willa's a little nervous about what Joe is planning to do with that cabinet, but we're both confident she'll like what he comes up with. It's going to take a couple weeks for Joe to put something together. In the meantime, we've come up with some unexpected issues on the North Providence house, and he and I have decided to divvy up the work to keep both of these projects on track. So, it'll just be me managing this project now."

"Huh," Hannah said. She twisted her head towards Julia and raised one eyebrow. "Wonder what happened behind the scenes there. Did Tony tell you?"

"He said he'd told Willa about me and warned Joe to back off. This must be around that time."

And Joe, to his credit, had tried hard to stay away. He'd told Julia of his struggles, how much he'd fought to rid himself of his feelings for Willa.

So much of their conversation on that horrible day was still a blur, but Julia did remember the agony in his voice when he'd said: *"This is the first time I've ever gone back on a promise I've made. The thought of hurting you has been tearing me apart."*

"I can see how this series is going to be a big hit with the ladies," Hannah said, tugging Julia out of her thoughts. "Tony is serious eye candy. Look at the way he's swinging that hammer."

Julia returned her focus to the screen, watching as Tony nailed down some boards on a staircase and then helped his crew install drywall. The scenes were moving quickly now as the voiceover narration explained the various stages of the project and how smoothly things were coming along.

"He's so natural in front of the camera," Hannah went on. "Joe was kind of stiff, but Tony looks like he's been doing this for years."

"It was his idea to do the show. Joe went along with it. He's always put Tony and Sylvie first."

Hannah made a noncommittal sound in response as they watched Tony and Willa strolling through an appliance store. Next they visited a furniture warehouse. As the segment continued, Julia found her eyes drawn more towards Tony than to Willa. He really was a natural, like Hannah said. He had a confident, take-charge demeanor that was balanced with a genuine, good-natured charm. He seemed to light up the screen.

He hadn't always been so good-natured, she thought, recalling some of the arguments she'd had with him during his teenage years. He was the only person she'd ever fought with like that—fierce, verbal battles that made her face red and her heart race out of control.

Tony's Uncle Nick had put a stop to Tony's belligerence towards Julia when Tony was eighteen. Nick had been on leave from a tour of duty in Afghanistan and was staying at the Rossetti house. Julia was over at their house one afternoon preparing dinner. She heard Tony's car pulling into the driveway; he was home from school. He strolled into the kitchen, tossed his backpack on the table and yanked open the refrigerator door. He stood there in the opening as he drank milk straight from the carton, his head thrown back, his profile smirking.

It was clearly intentional. He knew how much this bothered her; she'd asked him too many times before to use a glass. He was a senior in high school, full of testosterone and feelings of male invincibility.

"Tony," she asked quietly. "Please use a glass. And close the door. You're letting all the cold air out."

He took a few more gulps before closing the lid on the carton and putting it back on the top shelf of the refrigerator. His movements were slow and deliberate as he closed the door and turned to face her. "What does it matter to you? You're not the one paying the bills."

"And neither are you. It's Joe who's working his ass off to keep the lights on around here."

Something washed across his features that looked like shame. But it vanished as quickly as it appeared. His mouth twisted. He took a step closer to her. "I've got a job. I help out where I can. When are *you* going to get a real job, princess? When are you going to stop playing house with us and go out into the real world?"

She straightened her shoulders, forcing herself to stand firm and to not reveal how much his words hurt. He was a few inches taller than she. She was suddenly aware, as she'd never been before, of how much his body had filled out in the last year or two. His shoulders were broader, his arms more muscular. The planes and angles of his face were more chiseled. He was becoming a man. But he was behaving like a boy.

"I *have* a real job."

"Yeah. Working for your mom and dad. The interview process for that must have been *real* grueling. Why aren't you at your job now? I'm eighteen. I can take care of Sylvie. We don't need you here playing mother anymore."

She put her hands on her hips. As much as she tried to keep an even keel, she couldn't prevent her voice from raising a couple of decibels. "You may be eighteen. But you still act like you're twelve. And you can gripe all you want about what I'm doing here. I'm not leaving. I *am* your brother's girlfriend. I have a right to be here."

His face reddened. His eyes narrowed in a look of resentment. "You're just a convenience. Joe doesn't have time to find a *real* girlfriend."

Her mouth fell open. Her heart constricted with pain. It was the most hurtful thing Tony had ever said to her. In the past, she'd been able to brush aside his antagonism, maintaining sympathy for the fact that he'd lost both of his parents in a tragic fire when he was only twelve years old. His antipathy towards her was normal and understandable. He had put up boundaries a few weeks after the funeral, making it very clear to Julia that she was not and never would be a replacement for his mother.

And she'd respected those boundaries. She'd been

able to work around the bad times with him because there had been some good times, too. Like the time when he was fourteen, and they'd all gone to Narragansett Beach, and he'd tried to teach her how to surf. He'd been very patient with her awkward attempts to stay upright on the board; there'd been a lot of teasing and laughter that day. Or the time when he was sixteen and going on his first real date. He'd asked her for advice on what to wear and how to behave like a proper gentleman. Or that hot August Saturday afternoon, just before he turned eighteen, when the two of them had been waiting for Joe while he met with a client in South Kingstown. They'd had a few hours to kill, and Tony decided to take her crabbing. They'd stopped at a local market to buy a pack of chicken wings and some twine and then drove to one of Tony's secret fishing spots along Point Judith Pond, a place that his father had taken him and Joe to fish when they were boys.

He'd parked the car in the shade at the end of a bumpy, unpaved, densely tree-lined road, retrieved their purchased items from the trunk along with a fishing net and a bucket and led her down an almost invisible path to the water's edge. There hadn't been anyone else around. The day had been hot and humid. Julia remembered that she'd been wearing a white skirt and matching tank top in cool cotton. Deciding she didn't want to get dirty, she'd strolled out to the end of an old, wooden pier while Tony searched along the muddy shoreline for some long sticks.

When he joined her on the pier, they worked in companionable silence, attaching lengths of twine to one end of each of the sticks he'd found, then tying a chicken wing to the other end of the twine. They set up four rigs in all, pushed the sticks into grooves between the narrow wood slats of the pier and then threw the chicken wings out into the water, watching as the bait sank to the bottom. Tony pulled in the slack on each of the lines and then kicked off his flip-flops and sat down, legs dangling off the edge of the pier. Julia removed her sandals and sat down beside him.

"Now we wait," he said, sounding relaxed and happy.

She remembered that they hadn't talked much. They'd simply enjoyed the sunshine and the cool water lapping against their feet. She remembered wishing that she could have moments like these with Joe; he was always so busy—working long, backbreaking hours to keep the family business running and his brother and sister fed and clothed.

She remembered the twine on the stick closest to her starting to dance and Tony's calm voice in her ear as he helped her slowly and steadily pull the string towards the pier. As the blue crab came into sight, its claws digging possessively into the chicken wing, Tony told her to keep pulling while he grabbed the net and prepared to bag their catch. He lay on his stomach next to her, arm outstretched.

"Pull up!" he shouted.

She gave the string a firm yank, and Tony scooped the net under the crab. He gave a buoyant whoop of laughter as he captured the crab and lifted the net. She shrieked when he brought the net too close to her. He'd toyed with her for a few seconds, pretending he was losing control of the net, and she'd scrabbled backwards on her bottom along the pier, laughing and pleading with him to stop at the same time.

That had been a fun afternoon. Tony had been so nice to her, almost sweet.

Now, standing in the kitchen that suddenly felt confining, she couldn't think of a word to say to his cruel remark. She felt pinpricks of tears threatening to fall. Her mouth wobbled.

Tony's dark eyebrows shot up; his harsh features melted into a contrite expression. But it was too late for apologies. Nick, who must've been standing in the hallway and listening to their argument, came storming into the room, all six feet, five, muscle-packed inches of him. He grabbed Tony by his shirt collar and hauled him out the backdoor to the fence-enclosed yard where he'd proceeded to beat the crap out of his nephew. Nick's movements were controlled, his expression taut and grim as he pounded his fists into Tony's face and then across his shoulders, back and ribs when Tony hunched over in an effort to avoid the punches.

Julia had stood on the doorstep, hands pressed to her face as she watched in shocked silence. She wasn't used to violence. Being an only child, she'd lived a fairly sheltered life and avoided any kind of physical altercation. At the same time, she felt relieved that Nick had stepped in. Joe was so seldom home; he'd never witnessed Tony's antagonism towards Julia. And she'd never shared it with him because she didn't want to burden him. Joe already had too much on his plate.

Tears streamed down her face as she watched Tony take his punishment. But when he began to groan and plead for mercy, she called out beseechingly, "Stop, Nick! Please stop. That's enough."

Nick gave Tony a harsh shove to the ground, then lifted him back up again by his collar. He got in close to his nephew's face and said calmly and coolly, "If you ever treat that sweet lady with disrespect again, you can consider this as just a dress rehearsal. Next time, I won't pull any punches."

He released Tony's collar and stalked back into the house. Tony swayed on his feet, looking ready to pass out. Blood streamed from his nose and one corner of his mouth. Julia ran towards him but halted less than a foot away as he held out a stopping hand. "Don't," he said in a choking voice.

"Come into the house. I'll put some ice on your face."

"No. I'll do it myself."

She didn't realize that she was still crying until Tony reached out and touched her cheek with a shaking hand. His fingers traced her damp skin. His light brown eyes glistened with his own tears. He looked absolutely shattered. "I'm sorry, Julia," he rasped. "I'm sorry I've been such an asshole to you. I promise I'll never make you cry again."

And he hadn't.

Strangely, though, over the years, she'd sometimes found herself thinking back on those arguments and recalling how energized and animated she'd felt. Of everyone she'd ever known in her thirty-three years, Tony was the only person who'd been able to stir such passionate depths of emotion inside of her.

Sometimes she missed that side of her nature.

"Jules. *Jules*! Are you even paying attention to this? After this commercial, they're going to Joe's cabinet shop to see what he's done with that wall unit."

Hannah's face loomed in front of Julia, tugging her out of her vodka-soaked reverie.

"Huh?"

"Okay. No more shots for you. You look ready to crash."

Julia blinked. "I'm fine. Jus' thinking about Tony."

"Tony? Why?"

"He's never made me cry. He did once. A long time ago. But not anymore."

Hannah patted Julia's hand. Her own voice was slurred. "That's good. That's good. No one should make you cry."

"Joe made me cry."

"Yeah, he did. But you're gonna move on. You're gonna find a guy worthy of your love."

"Joe wasn't worthy."

"No… *Look* there he is."

Joe's face loomed on the screen. He looked tired and a little grim as he explained that he was fabricating two different furniture pieces out of the kitchen wall unit. One would go in Willa's new kitchen; the other would go in the bakery Willa was planning to open on Thayer Street.

And then Willa was entering Joe's cabinet shop, and he was showing her a wooden bench he'd built, and he put his hand real close to hers on the bench— their pinkies almost touched—and they looked at each other like the cameras weren't even in the room.

"What's wrong with *me*?" Julia wailed.

Hannah turned off the television and tossed the remote aside before dragging Julia into a fierce hug and rocking her back and forth. "There's not a damn thing wrong with you, honey."

"Then why did he leave me? Why did he choose

her? Wasn't I good enough for him? Aren't I pretty? Aren't I kind and smart?"

Julia felt Hannah's hand on her back, rubbing, soothing. "Of course you are, sweetie. Of course you are."

"I *am* kind and good. I've been a good girl all my life. My mom and dad's perfect little girl."

"*Shh*. Let it go, Jules. You just gotta let it go."

Julia yanked out of Hannah's embrace and gave her friend a fuming glare. "Let it go? Let it *go*? Like I'm some kind of animated cartoon character? What the *fuck*! I've been dreaming about my wedding since I was a little girl, since I was five years old and hit Joe on the head with my p-plastic shovel in the sandbox. My m-mom told me that same day that I was going to marry him one day. He was supposed to be t-the *one*! And he just dropped me like that." She tried to snap her fingers but failed. She flung her hands in the air instead. "He didn't give me any w-warning. Nothing! It was like I was a defective p-purchase he wanted to return for a refund!"

"That's not true. You can't think of yourself like that. He told you the reasons why…"

"Like what reasons? Like putting himself first for a change? As if I was just someone he'd taken for granted all this t-time? Like I was just the girl he'd settled for because he couldn't find his dream girl? What if we'd already been m-married when he met her? Would he have dumped me even then?"

"No. Not Joe. He would've stuck by your side. You know that."

"And he would've been absolutely m-miserable." Julia felt hot tears rolling down her cheeks. She swiped them away and rubbed her nose.

Hannah lifted a corner of the throw and dabbed at Julia's face. "We've had this same conversation too many times, sweetie. You're just torturing yourself. That's what I mean when I say let it go."

Julia took several hiccupping breaths. She tugged the throw out of her friend's hands and wrapped it around her shaking body. She fell sideways on the couch and curled her knees towards her chest. "I'm so tired. I don't know what I'm saying anymore. I get that he loves her. I get that she's his one. But he was *my* one... Wasn't he?"

Hannah stood up from the couch and pulled the throw across Julia's legs. She lifted Julia's head and propped a pillow beneath it. She brushed one hand down Julia's cheek. "Go to sleep. I'll be here in the morning. We'll go for a long walk. Talk when our heads are clear. Okay?"

"Okay."

Julia watched with bleary eyes as her friend walked to the bedroom, turning off the light as she left.

Alone in the darkened living room, Julia tried to tamp down the snippets of the conversation she'd had with Joe on that horrible, awful day, but they refused to stay put.

"What if you'd met her after we got married?"

"I was already having reservations and doubts before I met Willa. I couldn't have gone through with the wedding, regardless. I should never have asked you to marry me in the first place. It wasn't fair to you."

"Why? Wasn't I good enough for you?"

"No. No, Julia. Don't think of yourself like that. You are a sweet, kind and beautiful woman. You've always been my best friend. But I've finally realized that that's all you can *be. I know I'm being a selfish prick right now when I ask you if*

we can keep our friendship going. You're part of my family, Julia. You always have been. I don't want to lose that. And I know that there's a guy out there who'll be a much better husband for you than I could ever be. Don't give up on that dream because of what's happened with us. I'm not going to let you."

Sweet. Kind. Her parents' perfect little girl.

What had that gotten her?

Nothing but heartbreak.

At least now she was finally able to fully acknowledge and accept a truth that she'd secretly hoped was a temporary madness on Joe's part. He really did love Willa. It was there, in living color, for the entire world to see. He wasn't coming back to Julia. Ever.

It was time to move on.

Chapter Two

"He's been out there for ten minutes now. Doesn't look like he's calmed down much. I'll go talk to him."

"Give him a few more minutes," Willa advised, coming to stand beside Tony at the kitchen island where they could both observe Joe pacing back and forth on the screened back porch. "He's been on edge for the last week. He was worried about how the episode would be edited. He didn't want too much emphasis on me and him."

Tony gave a curt shake of his head. "Veronica pulled a fast one on us," he said grimly, referring to the field producer of the television series. "All those damn close-ups."

"I think it was unavoidable. Things were more obvious than we realized."

Tony pulled his eyes from his brother to focus on the woman standing beside him. He liked Willa; he had from the beginning. She and Joe made a good match. "How do *you* feel?"

She sighed heavily. "I'm relieved that it's finally aired. It's all the girls have talked about for the last month. But I'm just as worried as Joe about hurting Julia further. Neither one of us wanted that."

"I think she would've been hurt no matter how the

episode was edited." Tony took a swig from the bottle of beer he'd been nursing for a while and propped one hip on the counter to face Willa directly.

"Do you think she watched it?" Willa asked.

"I know she did. She told me she was going to."

Willa gave him a searching look. "The two of you talk often?"

"I see her at least once a week."

"But she still won't talk to Joe. She hasn't returned any of his calls."

"Can you blame her?"

"No. But it's bothering him so much." She glanced towards the porch again, her expression tautening with concern. "I hate to see him this way."

Tony felt the same. "These are unusual circumstances. Had it been anyone other than Julia…"

Willa glanced up at him. "She's part of your family. I get that."

He set his beer on the counter so that he could pull Willa in for a brief hug. "And so are you."

She hugged him back and then stood back so she could look him in the eye. She smiled. "Thank you."

"Things will work out, Willa. I know it."

"How's that coffee coming along?" Collette Fournier, Willa's next-door neighbor, asked as she walked into the kitchen.

From the living room came the sound of female chatter and laughter. All the girls—Audrey, Shirley and Mercy—had come to Willa's house to watch the show. They were Collette's best friends and had quickly become Willa's, too. Both Joe and Tony had been taken into their fold; the fifty-something women enjoyed pretending they were the fussy aunts that the brothers had never had.

Sylvie, Joe and Tony's little sister, was there, too. She'd graduated with honors from Johnson and Wales University in May and was now working fulltime as Willa's assistant manager at the bakery Willa had opened on Thayer Street in Providence back in June.

Tony's features relaxed in a grin as Collette sidled up next to him and playfully nudged him in the ribs with her elbow. He couldn't help but smile every time he was around her. She had one of those loud, effusive personalities that were very prevalent among women of her generation in the North Providence neighborhood where he'd grown up. She reminded him a little bit of his mother, who'd been strong and fearless in addition to being very protective of her children. He felt a little twist of pain in his heart; not a day went by that he didn't think of his mother at some point. "How you doin', Collette?" he asked, laying his Little Rhody accent on thicker than usual. "How does it feel to be a TV star?"

Collette beamed. "I looked good on there, didn't I."

"You were the highlight of the show."

"Sylvie says I should open a Twitter and Instagram account for all the fans I'm going to have. She's going to show me how."

"Go for it."

Collette tugged her cellphone from her pants pocket and handed it to Willa. "Take our picture, hon. This'll be my first post, or whatever you call it. Me and Mr. Tall, Dark, Sexy and Handsome here. My co-workers are going to be so jealous."

Tony's grin widened as he threw an arm around

Collette's shoulder and allowed himself to be posed to the older woman's satisfaction. After Willa took a couple of shots, he glanced towards the porch. Joe was no longer in sight. "Think I'll go outside for a while," he said to the ladies, giving Willa a speaking look.

She nodded. "I'll have dessert ready in a half hour. Collette, can you help me with the whipped cream?"

Tony stepped onto the back porch and looked around. Through the screen, he caught a glimpse of Joe walking around the corner of the house towards the front yard. Tony pushed the screen door open and set out after him.

It was a warm September night, just one week after Labor Day. The sun had gone down a couple of hours ago. As he moved away from the light streaming from Willa's house, it took a few seconds for his eyes to adjust to the mid-evening dark. Then he saw Joe walking down the driveway towards the street. Tony quickened his pace until he came abreast of his older brother.

Joe gave him a sideways look but didn't speak. He only nodded to the left, indicating the way to the main road that led to Conimicut Point Park.

They walked in silence for a while, keeping their eyes on the road. Aside from the occasional passing car, the neighborhood was quiet. Dinner smells wafted in the air, combining with the scent of the salt marsh and the fainter scent of sea lavender.

It'd been a long time since he'd been alone with his brother like this, Tony reflected. They'd both been working nonstop on the television series since April. There'd been six projects in total, each one with unique challenges that had piled on extra hours right up until the final shoot that had taken place in early August. This was on top of a few other projects their construction company had taken on that weren't related to the show. Business was better than it had ever been, and they'd been able to hire a couple of project managers plus additional crew to help offload some of the strain.

When Julia and Joe had still been together, Tony had seen both of them almost every day. He, Joe and Sylvie shared the three-decker house in North Providence where they'd been raised. Julia's parents, Tom and Diane Kelly, lived next door. When Frank and Sarah Rossetti had been killed in a warehouse fire fifteen years ago, Diane and Julia had taken on most of the cooking and cleaning for the orphaned Rossetti siblings. Although Joe and Julia's romantic relationship had been off and on over the years, there had been very few occasions where Julia hadn't joined the Rossetti clan for dinner or just to hang out with them.

But Joe had moved in with Willa in July. And Julia hadn't been back to her parents' house since May. When Sylvia wasn't working at the bakery, she was off with her friends, enjoying her early twenties to their fullest, as she should. Most nights, when he wasn't catching up on paperwork at the office, Tony spent alone in a quiet house. Much of his eating these days was of the take-out variety. As he sat at the kitchen table, surrounded by empty chairs, his thoughts— more and more often—centered on Julia. In his mind's eye, she was sitting across from him, her blond hair framing her lovely, heart-shaped face, her amber eyes smiling at him.

"When was the last time you saw her?" Joe asked,

31

as if he'd been reading Tony's thoughts.

Tony cleared his throat. "Last week. Helped her move some furniture."

"Yeah? Where?"

"In her office. She's converted the back room into a conference room. Looks nice."

"Business has been good?"

"There wasn't much going on in August, but it's picking up again. She has some corporate functions lined up through December."

"Good."

They walked a few yards farther in silence. Joe kept his gaze straight ahead when he asked, "Does she... Do you two talk about me? About Willa?"

Tony kept his tone neutral. "Just once. Right after she came back from San Diego. She wanted my take on things. Did I know what had been going on. Did I think it was legit. That kind of thing."

"What did you tell her?"

"The truth. That I'd tried to prevent it. How hard you tried to stay away from Willa. Nothing you probably didn't tell her already."

Joe drew up short and pivoted to face Tony. He folded his arms across his chest and scowled. "Damn it. I wish I'd told Veronica what was going on. She said from the beginning that the wall unit would be the central focus of the episode. She could've edited things differently."

"That storyline and you and Willa go hand in hand," Tony pointed out. "I don't think there was any way she could've avoided it."

"I didn't want to cause Julia any more hurt or embarrassment."

Tony sighed. "I'll stop by her place this weekend.

Feel her out. It's been four months. It's time for both of you—all of us—to move on."

Joe gave him a measuring look. He seemed to hesitate a moment before saying, "You see her a lot then."

Tony shrugged, trying for nonchalance. "I used to see her every day before you two split. Sylvie sees her, too." He retrieved his cellphone from his jeans pocket and glanced at the time. "We should be heading back. Willa said she'd have dessert ready in a half hour. That was twenty minutes ago."

Joe shoved his hands in his pockets as he turned to head back to the house. Tony kept one eye on his brother's stern profile, one eye on the road.

After a couple of minutes, Joe cleared his throat before asking gruffly, "So... You're just being a good brother to her then."

Tony's steps faltered a little. He took a fortifying breath. "I don't think of her that way. I don't think I ever did."

"How do think of her then?" Joe persisted, nothing more than curiosity in his voice. "As just a good friend?"

"Maybe."

Joe suddenly grabbed Tony's arm, bringing him to a halt. He had a good two inches on Tony, but there wasn't anything aggressive in his touch. He only looked concerned, an expression Tony had witnessed many, many times since that devastating night when their parents had died, and Joe had taken on the dual role of both father and brother, more of the former until Tony had left for college. "Anything you want to tell me, little brother?" he asked quietly.

Tony held Joe's assessing gaze. He squared his jaw.

"Still haven't sorted it out in my own head."

Joe frowned. He looked a little uncomfortable as he said, "If it's something…more, I want you to know I'm okay with it."

Tony's startled laugh was abrupt. "Bullshit," he said succinctly. "Don't act so damn noble. You know it's weird."

Joe dropped his hand from Tony's arm. His mouth twisted in an acknowledging smile. "Okay. Yeah, it's weird. Aside from the fact that she and I have a sexual history…" He made a gruff sound. "She's my age. Six years older than you."

Tony straightened his shoulders. "Five and a half to be exact. About the same age difference as between you and Willa."

Joe shook his head. "That's different. I'm older than Willa."

"Age is just a number."

"And you don't have an issue with the fact that she was in love with me since we were kids?"

Tony felt a stirring of annoyance, almost on the verge of anger. "That's what she said anyway."

His brother's eyebrows lifted. "You don't think she was?"

"Of course she was," Tony conceded. "But there are different kinds of love, as you've recently discovered. And who planted that seed in her head—and yours—in the first place? Her mom."

Joe cocked his head to one side. His expression turned considering. "And our mom, too. They teased me and Julia about it constantly."

Tony felt his features relax. First, he hadn't anticipated this conversation happening tonight. Second, he hadn't anticipated Joe apparently taking things so well. Tony was still coming to terms with his feelings for Julia, feelings that he was only beginning to realize had been lying dormant for years. "Do you think the reason you finally asked her to marry you was because it was what Mom would've wanted?"

Joe heaved a deep sigh. "I don't know. Maybe. You know how your own memories of things can change over the years, become embellished or exaggerated?" He shook his head. "Lately, I've wondered if things would've been different if Julia and I had just been left alone when we were kids. Left to figure things out for ourselves, you know? How much of our relationship was simply the result of the power of suggestion, planted in us at a young age? Both Mom and Diane said we fell in love with each other when we were kids, and they took it for granted that we'd get married someday. Julia was so set on it. In the end, I went along with whatever made her happy."

"Yeah," Tony said gruffly. "I know what you mean. I made her unhappy once, and I hated the way it made me feel."

They stood in silence for a few moments. Joe looked down, scuffed the toe of his shoe on the ground. He cleared his throat, glanced at Tony again. "You're my brother. I love you. And I don't want to see you hurt. There's no guarantee that Julia feels the same way about you that you do about her."

Tony folded his arms across his chest. His voice was firm with conviction. "I understand that. It's a risk I'm willing to take."

"What about the fact that I've slept with her?" Joe pressed. "I was her first. That doesn't bother you?"

Tony felt his face redden. "*Jesus*, bro. You had to

35

go there, didn't you. Yeah, it bothers me if I think about it too much. But then I remind myself that *I* will be her last and her always." His voice turned flat, hard. "And that's the last time you and me are *ever* going to have that particular conversation."

Joe's laugh sounded relieved. "Fair enough." He held out his hand. "Let's shake on it."

When Tony returned his brother's handclasp, Joe tightened his grip and hauled Tony towards his chest for a man hug. He pounded his fist on Tony's back and then rubbed his knuckles playfully over Tony's scalp. "Good luck, little bro. I'll be here for you no matter what happens. Like always."

Tony squeezed his free arm tightly around his brother's back before abruptly letting him go and retreating a couple steps. He had to swallow down a lump in his throat as he held Joe's gaze. Their eyes spoke more than words ever could. "Thanks, man."

Joe nodded his head, agreeing to their silent communication. Then he waved his hand forward. "Let's get back to the ladies. I don't like to keep Willa waiting."

As always, Tony was struck by the lightness that entered his brother's voice when he spoke Willa's name. "How are things going between you two?" he asked as they strode briskly up the road.

"It's good. Hell, it's better than good. Some mornings I wake up and wonder if I'm living some crazy dream. I never imagined I'd ever meet a woman like her."

"Any talk of marriage yet?"

"Oh, yeah. But we both want things to settle down first. These last few months have been insane. Between our show and her bakery, there hasn't been time to think of anything else. But it will happen. Soon."

They turned onto Willa's driveway. The lights shone like a beacon from the living room. Through the window, they saw all the women sitting on the wraparound sofa. They were in a huddle, heads close together. Audrey was gesturing with her hands while she spoke. Collette was bobbing her head up and down in agreement. Willa looked skeptical. Everyone else was grinning mischievously. Shirley clapped her hands together with glee.

Joe came to a halt just outside the pool of light. He exchanged a look with Tony. "This doesn't look good."

Tony nodded his head in agreement. "What do you think they're plotting this time?"

Chapter Three

She was never going to drink alcoholic beverages of any kind ever again.

Julia took another sip of water, praying the aspirin she'd swallowed a few minutes earlier would work some kind of magic real soon. Her head had cleared a little during her walk with Hannah that morning, but she still felt groggy.

Good thing she didn't have any client appointments today. She'd given her two part-time assistants the day off. Fridays were typically slow unless she had an evening event. Right now, there wasn't anything on her roster until the first week of October. She'd set aside today to work on her quarterly budgets. But she wasn't making much progress.

It was also a good thing that her ground floor office didn't have the distraction of exterior windows. It was another beautiful September day. She battened down the very tempting urge to put up the closed sign and go outside to soak up the sunshine.

Both her office and her apartment were located in an older building on Westminster Street in Providence that had been converted into spaces for both commercial and residential use. Her parents had leased both the office and a third floor loft over twenty years ago when they'd expanded their home-grown event management business. Julia had taken over the lease on the loft eight years ago and had moved in soon after. In March of this year, she'd purchased the business outright from her parents so that they could take an early retirement. That had been the plan all along and one that she'd cooperated with wholeheartedly.

She loved her job. Providence had gone through a major revitalization around the same time the Kelly Event Management office had first opened its doors, and it was continuing to become more vibrant with each passing year. Admittedly, the event business had been a little touch and go over the last seven years after the economy had tanked. The Kelly's had taken on more social functions than they normally did until corporate events had slowly begun to pick up again. Julia had experienced a steady flow of work since January; she had no complaints.

Her office was in the busy heart of Providence known as DownCity. She lived and worked in the midst of an eclectic mix of retail shops, art galleries, salons, clubs, restaurants and theaters. To her, Providence didn't feel so much like a city as it did a big town. In fact, when most Rhode Islanders talked about "the city", they were referring to New York City, which was a three hour drive south.

When the weather was nice, Julia usually spent her lunch hour outdoors. She liked to eat at Grant's Block, a spot farther down Westminster on the corner of Union Street that had once been a building site but was now an open public space for businesspeople, college students, shoppers and the like to gather.

Usually, she brought her own lunch. On Tuesdays, she opted for the delicious possibilities offered by the various food trucks that lined up on nearby Weybosset Street.

In the summertime, Grant's Block was the setting for weekly outdoor evening movies, free to the public. Just three weeks ago, Julia and Tony had parked lawn chairs on the cement along with a huge crowd of others to watch Fred and Ginger dance across the silver screen.

Afterwards, Tony had asked her if she'd be interested in taking ballroom dance classes with him. He'd joked that he'd spent more time looking at his female partner's boobies than focusing on the lessons he and his classmates had been forced to endure back in middle school. "Wasn't paying that much attention to my feet," he'd confessed with a laugh.

She'd laughed along with him. "Boobies? That's what you called them when you were that age?"

"Either that or titties. Hey, I was eleven. So, what do you say? Classes start after Labor Day."

She'd said she was interested, but she regrettably had to decline a few days later when some new business came her way that would conflict with some of the class dates.

As much as she loved securing new clientele, she really wished she could've said yes to Tony.

He'd been so good to her these past few months.

After the break-up from Joe, she'd escaped to her Cousin Eileen's condo in San Diego for a few weeks. Eileen was a flight attendant and wasn't around much. She'd invited Julia to stay as long as she'd needed. The first week, Julia had spent most of her time in bed. When she wasn't crying, she watched television and ate too much salty junk food. The second week, she ventured onto the patio where she spent more time crying. But she ate less of the salty food, drank lots of water and slowly began to feel alive again under the warmth of the early summer sun. The third week saw more of the same, except for that one Friday night when Eileen was home on an extended layover and dragged Julia to a local bar that was a popular hangout for Navy personnel. Emboldened with one too many Jell-O shots, Julia had almost—*almost*—invited one extremely hot-looking officer to come back to the condo with her. He'd gravitated towards her the instant she and Eileen had walked into the bar; it'd been a much-needed boost to her shattered ego. She remembered thinking with drunken logic that there was nothing like dirty sex with another man to take her mind off the man she'd lost.

But she'd never been that kind of girl.

She bought a return ticket to Providence the very next day and sent a text to her mother to let her know that the flight would be landing at three-thirty the following afternoon. But it wasn't her mother who was waiting for her in the baggage claim area at T.F. Green airport. It was Tony.

Julia had frozen in place for a few seconds when she'd spotted his smiling face in the crowd. He and Joe shared the same dark hair coloring and olive complexion. But, while Joe's hair was thick and wavy, Tony kept his cropped short. Tony's eyes were a lighter, warmer shade of brown than Joe's, and he was a couple of inches shorter. Even so, he still seemed to tower over her as she'd drawn closer. Without a second of hesitation, he'd tugged her into his arms and held her close.

"Welcome home," he'd whispered gruffly in her ear.

She'd allowed her body to rest against his for a while, missing the sensation of being held by a man. She'd felt tears forming but had quickly tamped them down. It had been too public a setting to cave in to the emotions churning inside of her.

"What are you doing here?" she'd asked against his chest.

"I made your mom promise me she'd tell me when you were coming back."

"You mean you badgered her and finally wore her down."

He'd chuckled. "Maybe."

He hadn't questioned her when she'd asked him to take her to her apartment instead of her parents' house. He'd carried her suitcase up the two flights of stairs. At her request, he'd made a pot of tea while she'd taken a shower. When they were ensconced on her living room couch, he'd turned to her and asked her how she was doing. His voice had been so tender. She'd burst into tears and practically thrown herself into his outspread arms, crying her heartbreak and misery into his shirt until it had become soaking wet. He'd murmured soft, indecipherable words of comfort and rubbed his hands up and down her back. Afterwards, he had listened patiently as she'd put words to her feelings about what had happened with Joe. He'd answered all of her questions directly and honestly. Later, he'd made her dinner and then tucked her into bed. She'd slept better that night than any night in the previous three weeks.

Since then, not a week went by that she didn't see

him at least once. Sometimes he'd stop by the office out of the blue. There had been a few times when she'd called him with one request or another—little things that she'd used to ask of Joe. Like fixing the leak in her bathroom sink, or helping her hang up a heavy mirror. He'd even helped her repaint the walls in the bedroom. If he'd guessed why she'd decided to completely overhaul the bedroom, he hadn't voiced it aloud.

He'd asked her to come over to the Rossetti house on a couple of occasions, stressing the fact that Joe didn't live there anymore, but she'd refused. It was too soon. There were too many memories in that house.

These last few months, Tony had been her rock. Sometimes she worried that she was growing to rely on him too much, even more than she'd ever relied on Joe. She was a grown woman. She needed to stand on her own two feet and not depend on him so much...

A bell chimed as the front door opened. Julia glanced up from her computer screen towards the reception area of her office. A woman stood in the entrance. She looked familiar.

Julia stood up from her desk.

The woman spoke first. "I don't know if you remember me. I'm Audrey King. We met back in May. At that breakfast?"

Julia hoped her face didn't betray her sudden bout of anxiety. She didn't want to think about that particular day; it'd been the last time she and Joe gone anywhere together as a couple. It had also been the day she'd met Willa. "Yes," she managed to say, glad that her voice didn't betray her nerves. "Of course. How are you?"

"Crazy busy, now that the college kids are back in town. Business at my store has been nonstop."

"Right. You own that jewelry store on Thayer Street. I've meant to stop by."

It was a lie and both women knew it. Julia wasn't surprised when Audrey arched one fine eyebrow and pursed her mouth in a moue of disbelief. "I'd be shocked if you did but absolutely delighted to see you. Willa's bakery is right next door."

Audrey didn't mince words. None of her friends did. They were a brash group of women, possessing a self-confidence and bravado that Julia had found admirable and even a little inspiring during her brief time with them at the May Breakfast she and Joe had attended at Collette's invitation.

Audrey had a very sophisticated presence about her. Her figure was tall and slender, almost gamine. She was dressed in a simple black sheath dress that provided the perfect backdrop for the blue-toned costume jewelry—no doubt her own creations—that accentuated her slender neck and wrists and the creaminess of her skin.

Julia stood up taller. She was glad that she had chosen to wear her usual business attire today—a black skirt and blazer, paired with four-inch pumps that put her on eye level with the other woman. She acknowledged Audrey's words with a stiff nod of the head.

Audrey gave a little sigh. She closed the door behind her and moved farther into the room. "Don't worry. I'm not here to talk about Willa. I'm here for business reasons. I need someone to help me plan an event. Are you interested?"

Julia's eyebrows rose. "What kind of an event?"

"I'm introducing a new jewelry line. Something I've been working on for the last year since I moved back to Providence." She touched her necklace. "It has an ocean-inspired theme. I'm very excited about it. I want to host a party for my customers and prospects. Not at my store. The space is too small."

Julia shoved her emotions aside and became all business. She retrieved her electronic tablet from her desk drawer and then extended her arm in a welcoming gesture. "Let's talk in my conference room."

As she led Audrey into the conference room that Tony had helped her put the final touches on just last week, she asked, "Would you like some coffee or tea?"

"No, thank you." Audrey glanced around the room. "This is nice."

Julia had gone with a sage green, cream and gold theme, offset by an oval cherry wood conference table with complementing chairs. "Thanks. I just finished remodeling last week. Tony helped me move the furniture. Please, have a seat."

"He's a doll," Audrey said, taking the chair Julia indicated and placing her black pocketbook on the seat beside her. "All of us girls are completely smitten with him."

Julia sat down across from her and opened the notes app on her tablet. She cleared her throat. "I have a few questions before we go any further. How many people are you planning to invite?"

Audrey smiled. "At least a hundred, I imagine. Between my customers, my friends and others, it may even be more than that. Let's say two hundred to be safe."

Julia jotted the number down and then returned her gaze to Audrey. "And what dates are you considering?"

"As soon as possible. I want buyers to add this to their holiday inventory. It might be a little too late for that. But I think they'll be as excited as I am about the line. Can we aim for the third Friday in October?"

Julia swiped her fingers across the screen to access her calendar. "Would this be an afternoon event? Or evening?"

"Evening. I'm thinking from six to ten p.m."

"That day is currently open on my schedule. What's your maximum budget?"

Audrey flicked her hand. "Money isn't an issue."

Julia did an inward eye roll. "Right. But I still need some parameters to work within. There are all kinds of events. Were you thinking of something elaborate? Or more casual?"

Audrey tipped her head to one side, giving the question some thought. "A little of both?" she ventured.

Julia did a quick mental inventory of the venues she'd worked with in the past. And then a light bulb switched on in her head. Which surprised her more than a little; her brain still felt like it was taking a bath in vodka. "Don't you have a factory in Pawtucket?"

Audrey's face brightened. "I do."

"Is it the kind of space that could work as a venue for your party? Since you're introducing a new line and looking for new buyers, they might be very interested in seeing where the jewelry is made. You could have demos set up and maybe give tours. Since there won't be a venue rental cost incurred, this will give us more options for the catering and entertainment."

Audrey clasped her hands beneath her chin. She looked thrilled. "That's *brilliant*. I knew you were the best person to go to. Tony has raved about how smart and business savvy you are."

"He has?"

"Of course. He talks about you all the time. Just last night he was telling us how much he admired what you've accomplished since you took over this business from your parents."

"He did?" Julia felt a brief glow of happiness that Tony had spoken of her so highly. Then she swallowed. "Last night?"

Audrey's smile flattened into a look of remorse. "Oh, dear. Sorry. Yes, we all got together last night to watch the show."

It felt like a big, cold lump of lead had lodged itself in Julia's stomach. She didn't want to know. She didn't want to ask. But she did. "We?"

"Tony, the girls—Collette, Shirley, Mercy. Sylvie was there, too. And Joe and Willa, of course. It was at Willa's house."

"I see," Julia said, a rasp in her voice.

Audrey leaned forward, her expression curious. "Did you watch it?"

Julia nodded.

"That must have been difficult for you." The woman's tone was sincere; her face was kind.

Julia shrugged one shoulder. "It wasn't easy."

Audrey sighed. "I apologize for prying. Will this be an issue for you? Planning my event? Considering that Willa and Joe are my friends?"

"No." The conviction in her own voice surprised

Julia, compelling her to sit up straighter. Where had *that* come from? "No. I don't allow my personal life to interfere with my work."

Audrey looked relieved. "Good for you. So, it won't bother you that they'll be coming to the party?"

A new kind of energy infiltrated Julia's veins. Would she have answered differently had this conversation taken place before she'd watched the show? Probably. But she'd made a promise to herself before she'd fallen asleep last night that it was time to move on. Time to let go. "No. In fact, it's time I met them face to face. It's been four months."

"Good for you." Audrey's voice rang with admiration. "I like a young woman with a strong backbone. I'm guessing things haven't been easy for you lately."

Julia gave a small huff of laughter. "To put it mildly."

The older woman's expression turned shrewd. "Life has a way of shaking us out of our shoes every now and then, just when we're starting to get comfortable." Her eyes locked with Julia's as her voice softened. "When I was a young graduate student at RISD, I fell in love with a very successful local businessman. He treated me like a princess. I had the best of everything. I thought that he was the man I'd spend the rest of my life with. And then, out of the blue, he broke up with me. I was absolutely devastated. I thought my life would never be the same. And you know what? It wasn't. It was better. I don't think I would've done or accomplished half the things in my life if I was still with that man today. And, in hindsight, I realized that I wasn't in love with him as much as I was in love with the kind of world he lived in."

Julia frowned. "So, what are you saying? That I should be happy and content to be single for the rest of my life?"

"If that's what you want. I certainly am. Personally, I don't feel that a woman needs to be married in order to feel fulfilled and happy." Audrey shook her head. "But, no, that's not what I'm saying. What I'm trying to say, as trite as it might sound, is that everything happens for a reason. You may not see it that way right now, but later, maybe years and years later, you'll realize that the break-up with Joe was a gift, a blessing in disguise."

Hannah had said something similar a while back during one of Julia's pity parties. But the words seemed to resonate more strongly when spoken by this woman who had more age and experience to back them up.

Julia attempted a smile. "I get what you're saying. And I look forward to that day. But, I'm just not that far along in my recovery yet."

Audrey's smile was kind. She reached across the table and placed her hand over Julia's. "You'll get there. And, in the meantime, you focus on what you love to do. And you gather people around you who are supportive and loving. Who knows? Maybe one of those people will end up being the *real* true love of your life."

Chapter Four

Julia woke up on Saturday morning feeling more refreshed and alive than she had in months. After a vigorous workout on her elliptical machine, she washed her hair and then painted her toenails a vibrant shade of hot pink. The color matched her mood. She threw on a pair of khaki capris and a pretty, flowing cotton blouse in multi-shades of autumn orange that seemed to intensify the color of her amber eyes.

She was glad she'd gone with her gut and watched Joe and Tony's show. She'd faced her lingering doubts and questions head-on. Did she still feel hurt and bitter? Absolutely. But she wasn't going to allow those feelings to hold her down any longer. Audrey was right; Julia needed to surround herself with the things and the people that she loved in order to find the strength to move on.

Joe had been one of those people. Maybe down the road they could return to the friendship that had been the foundation of their relationship. She knew she'd have to see him at some point. To continue avoiding him and the situation would only put a strain on her friendship with his brother and sister.

Now, with Audrey's party, she had a concrete date

to work towards. There wouldn't be any surprises. She'd be prepared to meet Joe and Willa together for the first time with confidence and grace.

She was buttering a piece of toast when the doorbell rang. She peered through the peep hole, smiled and opened the door.

Tony braced one hand on the doorjamb and grinned at her. His warm eyes assessed her from her hair to her bare feet and up again. "Don't *you* look colorful. I like it."

She smiled. "Thanks. Come on in."

She walked towards the kitchen as he closed the door behind him. "I wasn't expecting to see you today," she called over her shoulder.

He followed her into the kitchen and leaned one hip against the counter, watching as she spread some strawberry jam on her toast. "I didn't have any set plans for the day," he said. "How about you?"

She mimicked his pose, facing him. She took a bite of toast, chewed and swallowed it down, before replying, "Not especially."

She felt a weird fluttering in her lower abdomen when his eyes briefly dropped to her mouth before lifting to hers again. What was *that* all about? She searched his expression, but there was nothing there except casual regard.

"Good," he said. "It's a beautiful day. Let's get out in the sunshine."

"And do what?"

"I have something in mind." His gaze landed on her blouse. "We might get a little dirty. Do you want to change?"

"That sounds ominous."

"Not really. You'll love it. Just don't want you

whining later that I didn't warn you."

"I don't whine."

He chuckled. "No, you don't. That's just one of the things I like about you."

She narrowed her eyes at him as she ate the remainder of her toast. She caught herself wondering what other things he liked about her. Then she gave a mental shake of her head. That was just her needing a boost to her damaged feminine ego. "I'll bring along another shirt if I need it. Sneakers or sandals?"

"Sandals are fine. Don't want to hide those pretty toes."

She rolled her eyes at him. "Save your flirting for another girl. You know it won't work with me."

Something seemed to shift in his expression. "No? Guess I'll have to try a little harder then."

As her brows knitted in a puzzled frown, his features relaxed into an easy smile. "Go get your shoes. And bring a sweater, too. It might be cooler where we're going."

"Where *are* we going?"

"You'll see."

She heaved a big sigh of consternation as she stomped past him and headed for her bedroom. But it was all in jest. She was looking forward to spending a day outdoors, and Tony was good company.

Since it was a Saturday, he'd been able to park his pickup truck around the corner from her building. He took her elbow in a gentle grip as he helped her climb up into the cab. Through the windshield, she watched him stroll around the front of the truck to the driver's side. He was wearing tan cargo shorts and a black tee-shirt that molded his chiseled torso like a second skin.

Eye candy, indeed, she thought, recalling Hannah's

words from the other night. She arched her eyebrows at him as he got in the truck, fastened his seatbelt and then turned the key in the ignition. "Whatever happened to that girl you were dating back in April? Dana? Danielle?" she asked casually.

He flicked a curious look at her before he donned his sunglasses and directed his attention to pulling out of the parking space. "Danielle. That fizzled out pretty quickly. She wasn't the brightest bulb in the chandelier."

She stayed quiet as he expertly maneuvered the truck through the downtown streets and eventually took the onramp to 95 South. He was a good driver—confident but not overly aggressive. He maintained speed with the flow of traffic as they headed down the busy highway.

"I bet now that the show is out you're going to collect some fan girls," she surmised, breaking the comfortable silence.

He grimaced. "Yeah. I hadn't really thought about that. Veronica wanted me to open a Twitter account. I'm way too busy to spend much time online. I agreed to do a couple live chats on the show's Facebook page, but that's it."

Julia leaned against the side of the door, angling her body so she could watch him as he drove. "Does that page have a lot of fans yet?"

"Thousands. It's crazy. People are starting to recognize me. Some strange lady asked for my autograph at Stop and Shop last night."

"Some people might find that flattering."

He grimaced again. "It's all right when it's the locals. Wasn't expecting girls to be mailing their panties to the office, though."

Julia gave a shout of laughter. "*What?* Has that really happened?"

His face turned ruddy with embarrassment. "Sadly, yes. I don't know why they think I'd find that even remotely tempting. I've always been more attracted to the old-fashioned kind of girl."

He threw a quick glance at her, but she couldn't read his expression behind his sunglasses. Nevertheless, she felt a curious, fluttery sensation pulse through her veins at the way his voice had lowered a decibel on that last statement. She looked away, forcing her attention on the road before them. She was glad to hear the casualness in her tone when she asked, "Any girl in particular?"

"Maybe."

She shot him a look. "Really? Who? Do I know her?"

"Maybe."

She gave a huff of annoyance. "You're playing close to the vest. That's not like you. You've always told me about your girlfriends before."

He shrugged. "It's still too early in the relationship."

"Would I like her?"

"I think so." His mouth tilted in a secretive smile. "She's a lot like you."

She had no response to that. She returned her gaze to the road, but her focus was inward. His words had stirred a reaction within her similar to the one she'd felt the other night when she'd watched him put his hand on Willa's back as they'd been walking up the staircase. Now she wondered if it wasn't resentment she was feeling so much as jealousy. Why should she feel jealous of this mysterious new woman in Tony's life? Maybe it was just because she'd enjoyed spending so much time with him these past few months. He wouldn't have as much free time for her anymore once he had a fulltime girlfriend. Yes. That explained it.

"So, how was work this week?" Tony asked, piercing her confused thoughts.

"Hmm? Oh, fine. Busy. You?"

"Same. But not as crazy as it was while we were taping the show. I can breathe a little easier for a while."

"Has the network picked up the series for next season yet?"

"That won't be announced for a couple weeks. But Veronica is pretty confident it will be."

She relaxed a little in her seat as he eased them back into their normal camaraderie. "It's going to be a whole new life for you," she observed, returning her gaze to him. "I'm so happy that you and...your brother and sister will finally have financial security. It's long overdue."

"Yeah." He smiled. "I wrote Joe a check last month for my share of the company. Now I can officially say we're business partners."

"Congratulations. But you know that didn't matter to him. It's always been your company, too."

"It mattered to me." His tone was firm. "Now everything is fair and square."

She studied his profile. She was struck anew by how much he'd changed from the boy she'd known.

In the early years, when his parents were still living, she'd merely thought of Tony as Joe's tagalong baby brother. From the moment he could walk, wherever Joe went, Tony wanted to follow. And because Julia was the girl next door and Joe's best friend, that usually meant Tony was chasing after Julia, too.

She could almost still hear his clear, piping voice as he raced to keep up with her, his little legs pumping furiously. *"Wait for me, Julia! Wait for me!"*

He'd been a sweet little boy, a born charmer. Since he was almost six years younger, she'd usually made him play the role of the baby or the student or the patient in the "Pretend" games she'd liked to play. He'd always willingly gone along, just happy to be with her and Joe.

But as she'd entered her pre-teen and teenage years, she'd put those games behind her. Her world revolved around her hair and her clothes and boys. She only had vague memories of Tony during those years, flickering images of him kicking a ball in the fenced-in yard between their houses or throwing pebbles at her window and begging her to come out and play with him.

Then came that horrible night when Tony was twelve years old, and the policemen arrived at the Rossetti house with the shocking news that Frank and Sarah Rossetti had lost their lives in a freak accident at an old warehouse Frank had been converting into commercial space. There'd been something wrong with some pre-existing electrical wiring inside one of the walls. The building had caught on fire; the blaze had spread too rapidly for the couple to escape in time.

Julia had been babysitting Sylvie that night. It was February, and Joe had left for college the previous September. Tony had been playing video games in the front room while Julia had been reading Sylvie a bedtime story. It was Tony who'd opened the door to the police officers.

She would never forget the look on his face when she'd walked into the front hallway—the absolute heartbreak and devastation. She'd pulled him into her arms, holding him tight as he'd wailed his grief. His lanky body had shaken with gut-wrenching sobs. He'd buried his head against her neck, his hot tears soaking her skin.

Memories of the ensuing days and months were still enveloped in a fog. Joe had dropped out of school and become the legal guardian of his brother and sister as well as the owner of Rossetti Construction—a role he'd never wanted. Julia and her mother had stepped in to cook and clean for the family. Julia had been working fulltime at her parents' business by that point, but she and her mother had arranged their hours so that Diane was available to help the Rossetti's in the morning fixing lunches and making sure Sylvie and Tony got to school on time—while Julia returned home in time to keep an eye on them afterschool and fix their dinner.

Although Julia and Joe had dated casually in high school, their relationship hadn't evolved into a sexual one yet. They'd shared a few experimental make-out sessions in their teens, but neither had been willing or eager to push things further. Her mother had advised Julia that it was best for Joe to start college without a girlfriend. "It's tough to manage a long distance relationship," she'd said. "Let him enjoy his college years freely. You two are meant to be. He'll come back to you when all is said and done."

Worry for her best friend had kept Julia waiting long into the night for Joe to come home from work.

He'd been thrown into a business that was constantly in a state of flux, dependent on the economy and the housing market. The company had been hovering on insolvency, and the insurance money collected from the fire had barely covered the bills. Joe put in long, backbreaking hours to keep things afloat. Julia had waited for him to come home each night—most nights he hadn't returned until well past midnight. She'd greeted him with a warm dinner and comforting hugs.

One night, not too long after the accident, those hugs had led to something more. Joe had taken her to his bedroom and made love to her. They'd both been virgins.

It was shortly after that when Tony's attitude towards her had abruptly changed. There'd been a bittersweet interlude where he'd been extremely affectionate towards her. He'd let her hug him when he came home from school or ruffle his hair as he sat at the kitchen table doing his homework while she prepared dinner.

But that had all changed almost overnight. He became cold and hostile, avoided her touches, even refused to look at her. When she'd asked him what was wrong, he'd said, "Stop acting like you're my mother and that this is your house. You're not my mother, and you never will be."

No. She'd never viewed herself as a mother figure in his life. Not even as a sister, really. Their relationship had been rocky throughout his teenage years. After Nick had literally knocked some sense into Tony, she'd enjoyed one peaceful summer with the Rossetti family before Tony had left for college. She'd only seen him sporadically during those four years, and that hadn't changed much when he'd started working at Rossetti Construction fulltime.

Her relationship with Joe had been on-again, off-again over the years. In their late twenties, they'd stopped dating for almost three years and saw other people. But even when they weren't officially dating, she'd still been convinced that she and Joe would end up together. Although she'd moved into her own place by then, she'd made a point to visit the Rossetti clan on a weekly basis, joining them, along with her parents, for family cookouts and celebrations.

Tony had been there, too, usually with one attractive girl or another—his flavor of the month, Julia had teased. She and Tony had eased into a friendship that consisted of playful banter, good-natured ribbing, and mock flirtatiousness. He was the life of the party, whatever the occasion, and he doled out his charm to every woman who happened to be in the room.

But she'd laughingly reminded him that his charm was wasted on her. Her heart was set on Joe; Tony would just have to find some other bird to lure down from the tree...

"What are you thinking about?" he asked her now, tugging her from her reverie.

She shook her head out of the clouds and sat up straighter in her seat. "Nothing in particular."

"Looked like some deep thoughts were going on in there," he fished.

"Just thinking about work. Oh! I meant to tell you. Your friend Audrey came by my office yesterday afternoon."

"Audrey King?" He sounded startled. "What did she want?"

"She's launching a new jewelry line. She's asked me to plan a party to kick things off."

"Really? Well, that's great." He gave her a quick look before returning his focus to the road. "Tell me about it."

She outlined the details, her enthusiasm growing as she shared her preliminary ideas of transforming Audrey's factory in Pawtucket into an underwater world, in keeping with Audrey's ocean-themed designs.

Tony beamed at her. "That sounds amazing, Julia. You always have the coolest ideas."

She glowed. "Thanks! It helps that I'll have a decent budget to work with. Audrey isn't sparing any costs."

"Will you need help with anything?"

"Maybe. She suggested you might come with me to take a look at the space. She's thinking of having some display counters put in."

"She did, huh?" There was something curious in his tone, but his next words were casual. "Yeah, I could do that. I think I have next Wednesday afternoon free if that works for you."

"I'll check my calendar when we get back to my place."

Her stomach growled, startling them both.

He laughed softly. "Hungry?"

"Famished. I only had a piece of toast for breakfast before you yanked me out the door."

He smirked. "Hang tight. We'll get you fed soon."

She hadn't been paying attention to where they were going. "Did we just pass North Kingstown?"

"Yep."

"Are we going to Narragansett Beach?"

"Nope."

"Scarborough Beach?"

"Nope."

She continued the guessing game as he drove along, even when she realized where they were headed. When he pulled into a parking lot off Sand Hill Cove Road, she gave him a happy smile. "I haven't been here since last summer. What a perfect idea!"

He'd taken them to Galilee, a fishing village on Point Judith and the site of the Block Island Ferry. She and her parents had come here at least once every summer when she was growing up. Last year, she and Hannah had taken the ferry over to Block Island for a girls' weekend.

"I haven't either," he said, sharing her smile. "I like it better after the summer crowds have gone."

They exited the truck and stood together in the unpaved parking area, looking around. He pointed across the street to Champlin's, a fresh seafood market with a restaurant on the second floor. "How about there? It's still a little before noon. We'll beat the rush."

"Sounds good to me."

She ambled alongside him towards the gray shingled building. As they walked up the outer stairs to the restaurant, she felt his palm settle against the small of her back. Something quickened inside of her. She didn't pull away, letting him guide her as they approached the order window. They studied the menu affixed to the wall.

"Think I'll go for a lobster roll and slaw," he said. "What do you want?"

"Clear chowder. And I'll have the coleslaw, too."

"I'm getting a beer. You want one?"

She had a very brief internal debate between keeping her promise to never drink alcohol again and the allure of enjoying an ice cold beer on a warm late summer day. "Sure. A pale ale."

He dropped his hand from her back and pulled his wallet from his rear pocket. "Go grab a table on the deck. I'll wait for our order."

She nodded. Glancing around, she noticed the inside dining room was only half full. The deck, shaded by a blue awning, was more crowded, but there were still some empty tables available. She snagged some napkins and utensils before heading outside.

She commandeered a picnic table and sat down, facing the water view. While she waited for Tony, she gazed across the harbor towards the cluster of houses and buildings that lined the shore of Jerusalem, Rhode Island. It was a pleasing mix of ramshackle beach shacks and more upscale dwellings. Wooden piers jutted out into the water. Most of the boat slots were empty; the commercial fishing boats had left hours ago. A leisure boat slowly cruised along the water towards the sea, rock music sounding from its stereo. The sky was powder blue with just a few puffy white clouds hovering in the distance. She inhaled the briny air and closed her eyes, savoring the smells of ocean and fish—fresh and fried—and the distant hint of autumn. The sound of the water lapping against the pilings lulled her into a sunny daydream.

"Falling asleep on me already?"

Tony's teasing inquiry compelled her eyes to flutter open. His arm brushed against her shoulder as he set a food-laden tray on the table. He sat down beside her on the bench.

"It's such a lovely day," she murmured.

He swiveled his head towards her. He'd removed his sunglasses. His eyes were soft on her face. "It sure is."

She blinked slowly up at him, caught in his gaze. There was that strange, quickening feeling again. She looked away from him, forced her attention on their lunch. "*Mmm*. This looks good. And you got my favorite beer. Thanks!"

She picked up the bottle and clicked it against his before taking a swallow. Then she set it down and dug into her chowder and slaw.

They ate in an easy silence, enjoying the food, the fresh air and the scenery. The Block Island Ferry traveled up the harbor, loaded with homeward-bound vacationers as well as islanders visiting the mainland. People lined the railings, many of them waving at the diners. Tony and Julia waved back.

Tony tossed his napkin on the tray and patted his flat stomach. "That hit the spot. Are you finished?"

She drank the last of her beer and set it down. "We should go for a walk. Otherwise, I'm going to fall asleep right here."

He nudged her lightly in the ribs with his elbow. "Lightweight."

She rolled her eyes at him before swinging her legs over the bench and rising to her feet. "If they could mix beer and sunshine into a sleeping pill, I'd never have insomnia again."

Concern touched his expression. "Still not sleeping well?"

She shrugged. "Better than I was."

His eyes rested speculatively on her face for a few

moments, but he said nothing further as he helped her load up the tray and clean off the table. After they'd both used the restroom, they headed outside. They walked along the breachway towards the ocean and then kicked off their shoes, carrying them as they strolled close to the water's edge on Salty Brine State Beach.

The beach wasn't as crowded as it would have been at the height of summer, but it was still very busy. Julia watched some children making sandcastles and thought of the happy times she'd enjoyed here when she was their age.

Memories of Joe drifted into her thoughts again. She was trying to remember if he had ever come here with her. She didn't think so. They'd seldom had outings like this. He'd simply had no time during those early years when he'd been fighting to keep the company afloat. And as she became more immersed in the event business, she hadn't had much time for days like this either.

Funny, she'd never given it much thought until now—the fact that she and Joe hadn't experienced many of the normal dating and courtship rituals that most couples did. They'd behaved like an established, settled couple right from the start. There had never been anything close to a courting stage in their relationship; she had never been wooed.

Tony grabbed her hand to catch her attention. "Let's go sit on the rocks. Watch the boats for a while."

"Okay."

He kept her hand in his as they retraced their steps to the breachway, and she let him. His grip was gentle, but she felt its underlying male strength. She missed holding hands with a man. When they reached the breachway, he released her hand so that they could put on their shoes before clambering over the rocks to the other side. They found a flat, dry surface and sat down side by side.

It was very entertaining watching the various outbound and inbound boats go by: large commercial fishing boats, recreational trawlers, leisure boats and the occasional sailboat.

Joe brought his legs to his chest and wrapped his arms around them. "I loved coming here as a kid. This was one of my dad's favorite places."

She copied his pose. "I miss him."

"Yeah." His tone was gruff.

She rested her cheek on her knees, her head turned towards him. "You remind me of him. I think you take after your dad the most. There's something around the jaw and the eyes. Joe has your mother's eyes."

He looked at her. "Do you know that's the first time you've spoken his name out loud to me since the day you came back from San Diego?"

"It is?"

"Yeah."

"I guess that's a good sign then."

His eyes sharpened. "Did you watch the show?"

"Yes."

"And?"

"I could literally see them falling in love. Part of me was hoping..." She faltered. She pressed her lips together and slid her eyes away from his.

"Hoping for what?"

She lifted her head, keeping her gaze forward. She shrugged one shoulder. "That it wasn't real. That it had only been infatuation. That he'd change his mind."

"You'd have taken him back?" His harsh voice was almost like a whiplash.

She flinched. She sat up straight. "Of course not."

"Look me in the eye and say that."

She swung her head towards him. "You sound angry. Why?"

"Just tell me that you wouldn't have taken him back."

"It's a moot point. He's not leaving her."

"Say it." His voice was low and terse.

She lifted her chin. "No. I wouldn't have taken him back."

His tense posture relaxed a little. "Good. My opinion of you would have dropped several notches if you'd said yes."

She felt a rising tide of anger, the kind of anger she'd only felt during those long ago arguments with him. "Don't be nasty."

"I'm just stating the truth. I don't like weak-minded women. It's not attractive."

"I'm *not* weak," she seethed.

His features softened. He unclasped his arms from around his legs and reached out to brush the back of his hand across her cheek. "No, you're not," he agreed, his husky voice grabbing her low. "You're one of the strongest women I know. But you've had your time to be miserable. Now it's time to move on. Be the Julia that I love."

She stared at him mutely, her thoughts and emotions all jumbled.

And then Tony took on his usual cheerful personality again. He removed his hand from her cheek and rose to his feet. He pulled his cellphone from his pocket and glanced at it. "It's almost two o'clock. How about we get an ice cream cone for the road? There's somewhere else I want to take you."

Chapter Five

What was the matter with her?

Julia shifted restlessly in her seat, keeping her gaze averted from Tony as they drove away from Galilee. She licked and nibbled at her vanilla ice cream cone, but she wasn't really tasting it.

She didn't know if she should feel angry with him for prying into her intimate thoughts or grateful that he was gently prodding her to move forward with her life.

It wasn't gratitude she was feeling. She didn't know what she was feeling really. It was all so strange. Something between them was changing. It was there in the air between them, almost tangible. She wasn't sure she liked it. She'd always been so comfortable with the adult Tony. He was fun. Charming. Easy. But she'd glimpsed his darker, more serious side today; one that she hadn't witnessed in years.

He began to whistle along with the classic Eagles tune playing softly on the radio. She flicked a glance at him. He'd finished his ice cream cone. He had his right hand on the steering wheel, his left arm propped on the window ledge. He'd rolled his window down. He looked happy, carefree.

Maybe she was reading too much into things. It

wasn't as if he'd never touched her before or told her that he loved her. He'd always been more demonstrative of his feelings than Joe, more tactile and vocal in expressing his love for his family and closest friends. But, before, the words had always been said in a friendly, lighthearted way.

It was probably only because she was feeling so vulnerable and needy that she was reading more in Tony's words and actions than what was actually there. She was missing a lover's touch, that's all.

She and Tony were simply good friends, maybe even best friends. Yes, she felt the same for him as she did for Hannah. They were the two people who had stood by her the most during these last few months.

She relaxed. She gobbled down the rest of her ice cream cone and cleaned off her fingers with a paper napkin. She pinned a smile on her face and put gaiety in her voice as she turned towards Tony. "Where are we headed now?"

He kept his eyes straight ahead. The corner of his mouth twitched. "You'll see."

"More guessing games?"

"It's not too far away. Let's stop here first." He slowed the truck down and turned into the parking lot outside a corner market. He flashed a brief smile at her as he exited the truck. "Stay here. I'll be right back."

She watched him walk towards the building entrance. Her eyes lingered on his trim backside, his tanned, muscled calves, the confident way he carried himself.

Stop it. Just *stop* it.

He returned a few minutes later and placed a bag

in the truck bed. "Not much farther to go," he assured her as he got back in the truck.

Less than ten minutes later they were turning onto a familiar dirt road.

Julia gave a soft gasp and leaned forward in her seat.

"Remember this place?" Tony asked, his voice a little raspy.

"Yes."

He pulled the truck under the shade of an elm tree and killed the ignition. "That was a good day," he said quietly, not looking at her.

He hopped down from the truck. She got out after him, watched him as he threw the grocery bag into an ice chest and hefted the container from the truck bed. "Need any help?" she asked.

"Grab that bucket and the net."

She followed him down the narrow dirt path towards the water. Everything looked the same and yet it was different. The colors seemed more vibrant. There was a different quality to the air and the water, a sense of anticipation, as if this place had been waiting for Tony and Julia's return.

What strange notions she was having today. She'd been feeling so sentimental these past few days. Perhaps it was nothing more than simply being away from work, venturing outside her normal, defined schedule and the focus on clients and responsibilities.

They walked out to the end of the weathered, wooden pier and set the supplies down. Tony turned back to shore.

"I can help you find some sticks," she offered.

His gaze flickered to her blouse. "It's a little muddy."

"That's okay."

They headed in different directions once they stepped onto the marshy ground. She found a long, skinny branch among the low-lying greenery and snapped it in half across her knee. She swiped her hands on her khakis, leaving smudges. She didn't care.

Tony was cutting twine into equal lengths when she returned to the pier. He handed her two lengths, and she tied one end to each of her sticks. He slit open the pack of chicken wings with his pocketknife. They baited their lines, set up the poles and dropped the lines into the water.

She flopped down on her stomach and stretched her arms towards the water so she could rinse off her hands. He lay down next to her and did the same. The water was cool and clear. She scanned the rocks and tree branches on the bottom, searching for movement in the shadows.

Tony scooted back onto his knees, grabbed the bucket and dunked it into the water. Then he poured it into the empty ice chest. He repeated the motion until the chest was half full.

"Feeling lucky?" she asked.

"Always."

He sat on the edge of the pier and dangled his legs over the water.

She moved back a little, still on her stomach, and crossed her arms on the warm, sun-bleached wood. She rested her cheek on her arms, relishing the afternoon sunshine kissing her face, her arms, the backs of her legs. "This is my favorite time of year," she confided softly. "There's something about September that makes me happy and a little sad at the same time. For me, it's more of a time for new beginnings and resolutions than January is. Maybe it goes back to that back-to-school feeling we had when we were kids, you know what I mean? We're getting organized again, getting ready for the winter. And that's the sad part, knowing there won't be too many more days like this before the snow arrives."

He smiled at her upturned face. "I know what you mean. I like this time of year, too. The humidity is gone. The summer crowd is gone. It's quieter. More peaceful."

"Do you come here often?"

"Yes."

He didn't expand on that.

There was a tug on one of the lines. Julia pushed herself to her knees and grabbed the net. "Can I do it this time?"

His brows lifted in pleased surprise. "You sure?"

"Yep. And I don't want you waving the net in my face like last time."

His teeth flashed in a grin. He tugged carefully on the line. They both watched the blue crab rise to the surface, clutching onto the chicken wing for dear life. "Hold the net out," Tony said.

She leaned forward with the net. He yanked the string up and over, gave it a shake. The crab wouldn't let go. Tony pinched the back part of the top and bottom of its body and tugged the crab loose from its booty. It fell into the net. "Drop it into the ice chest."

Another one of the lines began to shake. Working together, they hauled in four crabs in quick order. Tony watched them scrabbling along the bottom of the ice chest. "Not enough meat yet," he observed. "Let's try for a few more."

They kicked off their shoes and sat side by side,

eyes on the lines as they sipped at the bottled water Tony had bought. Julia tipped her face towards the sun. "This was my favorite memory of that day," she said. "Just sitting. Enjoying a rare moment of peace with you."

His brief laugh contained a hint of self-deprecation. "They were rare."

She gave him a direct look. "It wasn't easy being around you back then, you know. I always had to be so careful about what I said, the way I acted. After the accident, for a while, you were very sweet with me. I wasn't trying to be your mother. I just wanted to be your friend."

His mouth twisted in a regretful grimace. "I know. Things just got weird. I was twelve. Going through puberty. You were—are—a pretty girl."

She felt her face color. "What? Are you… Are you saying you were attracted to me?"

He shook his head at her disbelief. "Come on, Julia. What do you think? You're telling me you never noticed the way I was looking at you?"

Her brow knitted. "No. I only remember you avoiding me, pulling away from me. I just thought it was because of the mom thing."

"No. I never thought of you as a mom or even as a sister. I was embarrassed about how I thought of you then. My body was changing. I was too ashamed to talk with Joe about it." He tugged on his earlobe, looking a little abashed. "I got a hard-on practically every time you were close by. Even if you weren't in the room at all, and I just got a scent of you. I couldn't control my reaction. One night, I got up to get a glass of water and saw you and Joe making out on the living room couch. He had his hands under

73

your shirt. That visual made things worse. Every time I jerked off, I was thinking of you, the way your face had looked when he touched you. And that made me angry because you were Julia, my childhood friend, my brother's girlfriend. I shouldn't have been thinking of you that way." He shook his head. "It was all so confusing and complicated. I didn't want you around, and I wanted to be near you at the same time. So I lashed out. I was able to control myself better as I grew older, but there were still times when I'd catch myself lusting after you. I think antagonizing you was a way of distancing myself from those feelings."

Julia's heart was pounding hard, her emotions in turmoil for the umpteenth time that day as she observed the myriad expressions flitting across Tony's face while he made his startling and frank confession. "I never knew…"

"I'm glad you didn't. After Uncle Nick tore into me that day, and I watched you cry, I started pushing those feelings down. I focused on making you smile. Making you happy. You told me once that marrying my brother would make you the happiest girl in the world. So that's what I wanted for you, too."

She swallowed down the rising lump in her throat. "I did say that, didn't I."

She looked away from him and gazed, unseeing, into the water. He was quiet for a while, too. Then he cleared his throat. "So, what would make you the happiest girl in the world now?"

She pointed her toes and swooshed them in the water. "I don't think anyone could possibly be happy all the time," she said eventually. "It was kind of foolish of me to base all my happiness on being with Joe. I never really thought much beyond our wedding day, you know? That's where the fairytales always ended, with the prince carrying his new bride into the sunset." She lifted her face to the sun again, tamping down all emotions and sensations other than the feel of warm heat on her skin. She smiled. "Real happiness comes in seconds and minutes—tiny moments like this that you can store away in your memory and open up when you're feeling blue, you know what I mean?"

"Yeah." His voice was rough. "I know what you mean."

She took a deep breath and opened her eyes. She swiveled her gaze towards him. "Some of my happiest memories from back then have you in them."

His toffee eyes gleamed. "Oh, yeah? Like what?"

She waved her arm to indicate their surroundings. "This, of course. And the day you tried to teach me how to surf. And that time you and I and Sylvie went quahogging on the Cape." She hesitated. "Joe wasn't able to join us for most of those outings. I wonder if things would've turned out differently if I'd had these kinds of moments with him."

Something hard flashed in his eyes. Whatever he might have said then was disrupted by a tugging on one of the lines. "Here we go," was all he said as he pulled the line in.

They caught six more crabs before he called it a decent haul and tossed the leftover chicken meat into the water. They packed up and trekked back to the truck. He put the ice chest in the truck bed and gave the water a stir. "These should be fine until we get home."

They didn't converse much during the drive back to Providence. He turned up the volume on the radio.

She closed her eyes, feeling pleasantly tired after a day in the sun.

The warm sensation of his fingers brushing across her cheek stirred her awake a while later. "We're here," he said, his eyes gleaming in the dusky interior of the truck cab. "You up to sharing dinner with me?"

She rubbed her eyes. "Sure. Do you mind if I take a shower?"

He grinned. "You just don't want to help me clean the crab."

She wrinkled her nose with distaste. "Not especially."

"Wimp. What happened to the 'you catch 'em, you clean 'em' rule?"

"Do you want salad with your crab? And a yummy dessert after?"

"That's bribery and you know it."

She fluttered her eyelashes at him.

His laughter followed her up the stairs to her apartment. She left him in the kitchen while she made her way to the bedroom. She grabbed fresh underthings, a pair of black yoga pants and a pink sweatshirt from her dresser drawer before heading for the bathroom.

He had a kettle of water boiling on the stove when she joined him in the kitchen about thirty minutes later. He'd also set her small dining room table, lit a couple of candles and dimmed the lights. Jazz music drifted from the stereo.

She felt something tug deep and hard inside of her. "Is the worst over?" she asked, pretending the nervous edge in her voice had to do with the thought of watching him clean the live crabs before throwing them in the kettle.

He smiled. "The worst is over. They should be ready in ten minutes."

She retrieved salad fixings from the fridge.

"I like that sweatshirt," he said. "It almost matches your toes."

"Thanks. Pink is my favorite color."

"You are such a girl." His voice was soft, teasing.

She felt color rising in her face; she kept her back to him as she sliced some tomatoes.

"Do you have crackers?" he asked.

"In the pantry. Bottom shelf."

His body brushed against hers as he slid behind her to open the pantry door. From the corner of her eye, she watched him as he opened a box of Ritz crackers and spread them out on a plate.

When the salad was done, she melted butter in a saucepan. "There's a bottle of wine in the cabinet above the fridge," she said.

"Red?"

"Pinot Noir."

"Perfect."

He uncorked the wine with expert movements. She caught herself observing his long, calloused fingers, the dark hairs on his sinewy arms.

Stop.

He brought the bottle and two glasses to the table. "I'll let that breathe for a few minutes."

His arm grazed against hers as he came back to the stove and lifted the lid on the pot. "*Mmm.* These are just about done. Nothing like fresh blue crab meat that you've caught yourself."

He propped one hip against the counter, watching her as she stirred the butter. "Watching you right now makes me think of all the times you made dinner for us. Did you like that? Do you like to cook?"

She lifted one shoulder. "I can't say that I *love* cooking. Usually, I'm so tired at the end of a workday. I'd rather have someone else doing the cooking for me. But I didn't mind cooking for all of you. It was a satisfying feeling, watching you enjoy those meals."

"They were pretty good. Especially your lasagna."

She grinned. "I made that a lot, didn't I. It was one of the easier recipes."

"We ate sloppy joes a lot, too."

She laughed, glancing up at him. "Another easy meal. See? I'm not exactly a gourmet chef."

He laughed with her. He reached out to tuck a loose strand of hair behind her ear. His laughter faded as a soft light entered his eyes. "You're going to be a great mom."

She felt a kind of giddy, drowning feeling as she held his gaze. "I hope so," she said.

"Do you want a big family?"

"I always did. I think that comes from being an only child. I wished I'd had brothers and sisters to play with." Her mouth turned down at the corners. "I'd shared with Joe that I wanted to start a family right away."

"And he was okay with that?"

"Joe pretty much agreed to anything I wanted. Whatever made me happy."

Tony compressed his lips. He took a step away from her. "Seems to be a trend with the Rossetti brothers, doesn't it," he said with a wry tone.

He lifted the lid on the kettle. "These are done. Let's eat."

The remainder of the evening passed comfortably.

The mysterious undercurrents that had edged into his conversation and behavior throughout the day disappeared. They talked of insignificant, everyday things as they ate their meal. They joked about all the work that went into cracking and picking the crab to get a small amount of meat. He complimented her on the salad. She toasted his crab boiling skills. The bottle of wine emptied. The candles burned down.

After dinner, he washed the dishes while she whipped up some cream to dollop on scoops of the fresh mixed berries she'd bought the day before.

They carried the bowls into the living room and sat on the couch. They ate in cozy, comfortable companionship as soft jazz music floated around them.

"That was good," Tony said when he was finished. He put his bowl on the coffee table. He glanced at his cellphone. "It's getting late. I should go."

Something dimmed inside of her. "Do you have a busy day tomorrow?"

He hesitated. "I'm helping Joe set up his spray booth. He's been converting Willa's garage into a cabinet shop. He's moving out of the warehouse."

"Oh? I didn't know that."

"Yeah. It frees up some warehouse space we need. And..." He shrugged.

"He wants to be close to her."

She surprised herself at how easily the words came, without a hint of jealousy or bitterness. She really *was* moving on.

She stood up with Tony and followed him to the front door. He reached for the handle and paused. He turned to her. "This was a good day."

Their eyes tangled. His gaze contained some

mysterious light that she couldn't fathom.

She swallowed. "Yes, it was."

The air between them seemed to shift, to thicken with the intimacy that had hovered between them all day. He took a step towards her. He brought his palm to her cheek and kept it there as he bent closer.

Her heartbeat pounded in her ears. Her lips parted in a silent gasp. She stood still, anticipation sizzling through her veins.

Tony brushed his mouth softly against her forehead, his lips pliant and warm. He inhaled deeply as if breathing in her scent. Then he stepped back and reached once more for the door handle. His eyes were luminous, penetrating, as he gave her one last look. "Yes," he said. "A very good day."

Chapter Six

God, he wanted her.

He wanted to hold her closer than he ever had before, breathe in her sweetly intoxicating scent, bury his face in her long, silky hair, taste her luscious pink mouth and tongue, sink himself inside of her clinging, feminine warmth, feel her legs wrapped around his back as he thrust and thrust into her until he'd spent his desire deep inside her body and then did it again and again and again.

Had it merely been lust that he'd felt for her when he was a randy teenage boy? Now he wasn't so sure. Because he didn't just want her sexually; he simply wanted to *be* with her. To talk with her, to laugh with her, to make her smile in that sweet way that made her eyes sparkle like jewels.

Had he given his true feelings for her away today? Had he revealed too much? The rational side of his nature demanded that he take things slow, to ease her into the possibility of them as a couple. It was natural for her to be put off by the idea, normal for her to feel some awkwardness or embarrassment about moving from one brother to the next. He got that. And maybe it was too soon. Maybe she needed more time to get over Joe.

But he didn't want to give her too much time. She was vulnerable right now, easy prey. He didn't want another man moving in, taking what was his. But he didn't want to be her rebound guy either.

There was such a fine line.

How beautiful she'd looked today. Her skin had glowed in the sun; her amber eyes had glistened. Her face had flushed a pretty pink color. Her laughter had sung through his blood and entwined around his heart. It was all he could do to not touch her constantly.

Even so, he'd touched her more today than he ever had in the past. It was a kind of taming—getting her accustomed to touches that were more than friendly. There had been moments when he'd felt her looking at him differently, a new kind of awareness in her eyes. A few times, she'd pulled away. She'd seemed uncertain, cautious. He'd been aching to kiss her at the door. But she'd seemed to stiffen, so he'd kissed her forehead instead.

Had he revealed too much when he told her how he'd lusted after her? When he spoke frankly about his physical reaction to her? No. He didn't think so. Julia had told him once that she admired openness and honesty above all else in her relationships. He felt the same way.

When the time came for him to have her, to finally take her—and he would—he didn't want any secrets between them. There would be nothing between them at all, only naked skin on naked skin.

Christ. He had to stop this. He had to think about something else besides Julia, otherwise he wouldn't get any sleep tonight at all. He'd already jerked off in the shower. Now he was hard again. He hadn't felt this out of control since he was a teenager. How long had it been since he'd had sex? There'd been that brief fling with Danielle back in April. Five months ago?

He'd never had any problem acquiring female company. But none of his relationships had lasted very long. None of those women had held his heart the way Julia did. If he got his way, there wasn't going to *be* any other woman for him now but Julia. She was the only one who stirred his blood. Her. Only her.

His deep sigh carried resignation and anticipation. He reached under the bedcovers and touched himself. He wrapped his palm around his stiff cock and gave it a tug. His groan echoed in his lonely bedroom as her face filled his vision.

Julia. *Julia.*

He took a longer lunch hour on Monday so he could pay a visit to Audrey King's eponymous shop on Thayer Street. She was helping a customer when he walked in the door, so he waited in the background, tamping down his impatience as he pretended interest in the jewelry on display.

Ten minutes later, Audrey was closing the door on the customer and turning towards him. She was wearing a long, wispy scarf-like dress that swirled around her legs as she approached. Brightly colored baubles dangled and jingled on her slender wrists. "Hello, Tony," she said with evident delight. "What brings you here?"

"Julia says you stopped by her office on Friday?" He kept his voice calm. "You're planning some kind of event?"

"That's right! I'm so glad she told you. I may need

your help with some things."

He braced his hands on his hips. "What's going on, Audrey?"

She arched one eyebrow. "I don't know what you mean."

"Bull. You ladies are up to your plotting again. Just like you did with my brother."

"What are you talking about?"

"Come *on*. You think I'm stupid? Collette badgering me to invite Joe and Julia to that May Breakfast? I didn't like being your unknowing accomplice."

Audrey pursed her lips. "Oh. That."

"Right. That." He didn't raise his voice towards her, but his words were clipped and cool. "And now you girls are manipulating things with me and Julia. I don't need your interference. I'm doing just fine on my own in that department."

Audrey's smile was all-knowing. "Ah. So you *do* love her."

He felt something lighten in his heart as he said, "Yes. I do." He sighed, feeling some of his annoyance dissipate. "How long have you all known?"

"Since the breakfast. It was pretty obvious. To us, anyway."

He relaxed his stance a little. He folded his arms and leaned against the jewelry display counter. "What are you women? Witches?"

She laughed. "That's hilarious. I can't wait to share that with the girls. No. Just think of us as your wise old aunts who've had more experience in matters of the heart."

"Old? You're what...thirty-nine?"

She laughed again, her cheeks blossoming with

color. "It's impossible for you to not flirt, isn't it. I've noticed you treat every woman that way, regardless of her age or looks."

He shrugged. "All women deserve to be flattered for the amazing creatures that they are."

"Oh, you charmer. Julia is a lucky, lucky girl."

His forehead knotted. "You know, I hadn't fully acknowledged my feelings to *myself* back then. She was still engaged to Joe."

"Funny how it's all working out then isn't it."

He frowned. "It wasn't so funny for Julia."

"She appears to be on the mend. I think she's over the grieving stage. She's ready to move on. She even said she's fine with me inviting Willa and Joe to the party."

"She is?"

"Yes. And she seemed very pleased when I told her of how highly you speak of her work."

"She did?"

Audrey set her hand on his arm. She looked contrite. "Yes. And I'm sorry. We *have* been plotting. But I was feeling her out more than anything. I wanted to get an idea of what she thought about you. Maybe give her a subtle push in the right direction. Open her eyes a little."

Tony sighed. Great. Now he felt like a boy at a school dance, wondering about the girl who was giving him the eye across the dance floor, wondering if she was really looking at *him*. Did she think he was cute? He rubbed the back of his neck. "I'm worried I might be moving too fast," he confessed reluctantly. "We spent the day together on Saturday. At the end of the day, I got the feeling that she still thinks of me as a friend."

Audrey gave him a measuring look. "Well, then. Use this next month working on my party together to change her mind. The last thing you want is to get so firmly entrenched in the friends category that she won't ever think of you as anything else."

His mouth twisted wryly. "Right."

"Just don't let her get too comfortable around you," Audrey pressed. "A mama bird will feed and care for her young, but then she pushes them out of the nest. Julia needs that push."

Tony stood up straight. He wagged a finger at Audrey in warning. "Okay. But you all stay out of it now. Tell the girls. I appreciate that you care enough about me and Julia to help. But I want things to happen naturally. Not because of your conniving."

The older woman nodded. She held up three fingers. "I promise. Scout's honor."

His mouth twitched at her sincere expression. "You were a girl scout?"

"East Providence, Troop number four seven three."

He was still laughing when he walked into Pauline's Cookie Bar next door a minute later.

His sister glanced up from the cash register. "Tony! What brings you this way?"

"Busy?"

"We were this morning. Enjoying some quiet before the afterschool rush."

He braced his elbows on the glass display. "Willa around?"

"She left about ten minutes ago." Sylvie closed the register drawer and gave him a speculative look. "So, what are you doing here? This is out of the way for you."

He gave her a sly grin. "Cookies?"

She rolled her eyes. "What kind do you want?"

His eyes gleaned over the trays of cookies beneath the glass. "How about the macaroons."

He helped himself to a cup of coffee from the self-serve area along the side wall and brought it to the bar counter along the front window. Joe had built that as well as the cabinet that was anchored to the wall behind the food display. The cabinet, with its pretty stained glass center door, had once been part of the wall unit from Willa's old kitchen. Now its open shelves held framed photos of Willa's Aunt Pauline, the woman who'd inspired Willa's love of baking.

Tony pulled out the stool next to him for Sylvie as she approached with a plate of cookies. "How's business?" he asked.

"Good. It was a little slow over the summer, but things are really starting to pick up now that the college students are back."

They dug into the cookies and sipped coffee and watched passersby on the busy sidewalk. "This is strange," Tony said after a while. "We live in the same house. But I hardly ever see you anymore."

Sylvie looked remorseful. "I know. Sorry. I've been busy here. And I like hanging out with my friends. You remember Katie, right? I stay at her place sometimes. She'd got a really cool apartment near Hope Street."

"That's cool. I'm glad you're having fun." He lifted an eyebrow. "Any boyfriends I need to beat up?"

She blushed. "Nothing serious."

He gave her a speaking glance. "You're being careful?"

She smacked his arm. "Yes, *dad*. Geez, between

you and Joe…"

He grinned. "You'll always be our baby sister, even when we're all hobbling around with canes."

Her face softened. "I know."

When the cookies were consumed, he swiveled his chair around to face her directly. He cleared his throat. "There's something I want to run by you."

"Okay."

"It's about the house."

His sister frowned. "What about it?"

He cleared his throat again. He hadn't expected the words to be so difficult to say; he'd been reciting them in his head for weeks. "Joe's moved out. You're not there much. It's feeling pretty empty." He rubbed his jaw, hesitated a moment before barreling on. "I think it's time to sell the place. I haven't talked with Joe about this yet. I wanted to feel you out first."

She gulped. "Sell? You mean, move away from there…forever?"

He nodded. "You're going to leave permanently someday anyway. Get married."

"That's a long ways down the road."

"What if Joe and I helped you get set up in an apartment closer to here? You could walk to work and downtown. Wouldn't you like that?"

Her mouth turned down. "But that's the house we grew up in. The memories…"

He swallowed. "They're weighing me down, Syl."

She rested her hand on his arm. "I didn't know. Are you okay?"

"Yeah. It's not like I'm depressed. It's just…lonely there for me. The memories, even the good ones… I think they're just holding me back."

"You've never said…"

He shrugged, striving for nonchalance. "Yeah, well there it is. I'm a grown man. It's time to move out of the parents' house and get my own place. I've been looking at a couple houses in the Cumberland Hill area. It'll be an easy commute."

Sylvie considered his words. "Wow. This is a shock. I mean, I'm happy for you, I guess. I kind of get what you're feeling." She squeezed his arm. "Let's talk to Joe. But what do you think about renting the place instead? We could fix it up into three separate units, split the income between the three of us. The housing market here is still pretty bad. Besides, you could use the extra income to help pay the mortgage on your new house."

It felt like a giant weight was lifting from Tony's shoulders. He flashed a teasing grin at his little sister. "Huh. Guess you learned something in college after all."

She punched his shoulder.

He ruffled her hair, a gesture that had annoyed her when she was a kid. She gave him a baleful look, but he could see that she was secretly pleased. "Are you sure, Syl?" he asked softly. "You'll be okay with leaving that house?"

She nodded. "My memories aren't the same as yours and Joe's. I was only seven when Mom and Dad died. I don't remember them in the same way you do. I missed them. But I think it was a little easier for me to adjust. You and Joe and Julia made sure I never felt abandoned."

"You were easy to love." His voice was gruff.

"Were?"

He ruffled her hair again.

She scooted her stool away. "Knock it off." Then

her expression turned coy. "Speaking of Julia…"

Tony rose to his feet in preparation to leave. "Not you, too."

"What are you talking about?"

He gave her a warning look. "Sylvie…"

Her cheeks flushed. "It was Audrey's idea."

"Yeah, and I just chewed her out. You all need to back off. Things need to happen naturally."

"I just want you to be happy."

Tony pulled her into his arms for a bear hug. "I *am* happy. I've got a sweet little sister and a good brother."

"I want Julia back in our family again." Her words were muffled against his shoulder.

"So do I." He released her and stood back. His voice was firm and confident as he met his sister's worried gaze. "But it's going to be a different family. Better than it's ever been before."

Chapter Seven

"Han, things are getting weird. I don't know what to do."

"Talk to me, sister."

"Maybe it's all in my mind. Maybe I'm reading too much into things, you know? I mean, I've always liked him. But now I think I *like* him."

"*Him?* Who him?"

Julia wondered if Hannah could hear her gulp over the phone. "Tony."

"*Tony?*! Joe's brother, Tony?"

"Yes."

"Holy crap."

"I know, right?"

"That man is hot."

"It's your fault. You called him eye candy, and I've been looking at him differently ever since."

Hannah laughed. "So? What's the harm in that? Is that all it is? Looking?"

"It's the way I feel when I'm with him. Something has changed. I don't know if it's just me feeling lonely and insecure. I'm in a very vulnerable place right now."

"True. But you need to dip your toes back in the water at some point, girlfriend. Maybe this is just a signal that you're starting to open up again, ready to get back in the dating pool."

Julia cringed at the thought of doing the dating scene again. That was still a ways down the road in her recovery plan. She needed to focus on herself for now; she didn't have the desire or energy that was required in building a new romantic relationship. "I don't want to get out there yet. I like hanging out with Tony. But, before, it was just as friends. Now—all this past week—he's all I think about. And in a more than friends way. It's consuming me."

"Better than thinking about Joe."

"True."

"So, define what you mean by things getting weird."

"I catch him looking at me in a different way, in a more…physical way. And he touches me…a lot."

"Touches you how?"

Julia confessed the details of the previous Saturday's outing with Tony. "I've seen him twice since then," she added. "He's helping me with this event I'm doing for Audrey King. We went to her factory on Wednesday to check out the space. And then last night I went to his office to look at some designs he put together for these fabric backdrops I'm planning on doing. It's going to be this ocean theme with lots of swirly fabric in shades of blue to look like waves."

"Sounds cool. So…back to the touching…"

Julia felt a shiver of sensual awareness dart up her spine as she recalled Tony's touches. "He likes to put his hand on my back."

"Down low? Just above your butt? God, I love it when Sam touches me there. It's so possessive."

"And he'll tuck my hair behind my ear, or brush his fingers across my cheek. Or he'll just stand real close so his arm rubs against mine. When he hugged me goodbye last night, he put his hand on the nape of my neck and brushed his thumb there, real slow."

"And what did you do?"

"I hugged him back and said goodbye."

"He hasn't tried to kiss you?"

"I think he wanted to last Saturday night when he was leaving. But he just kissed my forehead."

"Did you *want* him to kiss you?" Hannah pried.

Even though her friend couldn't see her, Julia nodded her head. "Yes. I think I did." She released a deep breath. "And that's just wrong. He's my ex-fiancé's brother! He's almost six years younger than me. That would make me a cougar. I shouldn't be thinking about him this way. Am I misreading things? Is he just being his usual charming self?"

"Okay. First, a six year age difference does *not* make you a cougar. Second, from everything you've told me, I think the signals are pretty clear that he wants you."

"Oh, my God."

"How does that make you feel?"

"Flattered? Nervous? Embarrassed? Weird? Don't you think it's weird? I've had sex with his brother!"

Hannah's voice was patient. "It's only weird if you let it be. You wouldn't be the first woman who's slept with her ex's brother."

"And what if that *does* happen? What if I sleep with him and then we both realize it was a mistake? Then I'll have lost them both. There's no way I could show my face around that family again if that happened. And that would be heartbreaking. They *are* my family."

"I guess that's a risk you're going to have to take." Hannah's voice turned strident. "From everything you've shared, it sounds like Tony really cares for you. He's known you all his life, right? You've been friends for a long time. Is there anything about him that you don't like? That turns you off?"

Julia couldn't think of anything. Except... "He's always been a flirt. He's not a player, but he's never had a girlfriend for longer than a few months—that I know about anyway. What if I end up being just another notch on his bedpost?"

Hannah was quiet for a few moments. Then she asked, as if struck with a sudden notion, "Do you think that the reason none of his relationships have lasted is because he's been waiting for *you* all these years?"

Julia's heart gave an odd little flutter. "If that were true, don't you think he would've said something before Joe and I got engaged? No. Wait. He wouldn't have. He said something last Saturday about only wanting to make me happy. I'd told him once that marrying Joe would make me the happiest woman in the world." Julia frowned. Her tone turned bitter. "Just what I need, another noble Rossetti brother hiding his true feelings for the sake of keeping me happy."

"It's kind of flattering that they both think so highly of you, don't you think?"

"I'm not a princess. I don't want to be put on some pedestal. I just want honesty."

"Do you think you'd have broken up with Joe if Tony had told you how he felt?"

"No. I don't think so... I don't know. I was so

immersed in Joe, so focused on marrying him." She sighed. "In hindsight, I can see that my head was in the clouds. I was living someone else's dream more than my own."

"You mean your mother."

"Yes."

Hannah's voice was gentle, coaxing. "Maybe it's time you had a chat with her. I think you've been angry with her for a while, and you just didn't know it. You need to get that out of your system."

In the end, Julia couldn't do it. As she shared a pot of tea with her mother in the Kelly's cozy kitchen the following morning, she found herself reflecting on her growing up years and what truly wonderful parents she had.

They'd only wanted the best for her. Sure, she'd been a little spoiled. Her mother hadn't been able to have any more children after Julia, and she'd lavished all her motherly love and attention on her daughter. But her parents had also taught her to be industrious and self-sufficient, instilling in her the desire to make a success of her life.

She supposed it was normal for a mother to hope and dream that her daughter would find her own prince charming and happily ever after one day. Julia envisioned her mother and her mother's best friend, Sarah Rossetti, sitting at this same table years ago, drinking tea and sharing their dreams for their children. They'd both been pregnant at the same time. How sweet would it be if one of them had a boy, and the other had a girl, and that boy and girl fell in love and got married someday.

Had her mother's dreams gotten out of hand? Yes.

But that didn't mean that Julia had been obligated to go along with them. Yes, her mother and Joe's mother had planted the seed. But Julia had allowed it to grow. Especially as she grew older. She could've said no. She could've done more to make her own fleeting dreams a reality. She could've ventured beyond her neighborhood, beyond her comfort zone.

Things might have turned out differently between her and Joe if his parents hadn't died. She'd been placed—albeit, willingly—in the role of pretend wife and helpmate to a young man who'd been obligated to take on the role of head of household and family provider far too soon. Although she knew that Joe loved her, she wondered if that love might have stayed platonic, if maybe they had initially fallen into the physical part of their relationship simply because it had been a kind of healing for them both, not to mention convenient.

He'd been her first. In hindsight, that had been part of the whole mess, too. She'd always thought that the man she gave her virginity to would be the man she married—a notion in this day and age which she acknowledged most people considered old-fashioned.

When she and Joe had split up for three years, she'd dated other men. She'd had a long-term relationship with one of them. She'd never shared the details with Joe. She'd just assumed he would realize that the relationship had included sex, just as she'd assumed that she wasn't the only woman Joe had ever been with. In the end, that guy had proven to be too immature and lazy, riding on the coattails of his father's success. Maybe if she'd never known Joe she wouldn't have harped on those faults as much; when it came to hard work and integrity, both Joe and Tony set the bar.

Funny, she'd almost overlooked Tony in that regard these past few years. Peeling back the layers of his boyish charm and easy manner revealed a man who worked just as hard as his brother, a man who'd stepped up to the plate to help keep the family business going and who'd had the foresight to move it a step further. It had been Tony's idea to send in audition tapes to the HOME network for the television series, Tony's ambition that had finally pulled the company out of the red once and for all.

He was a good man.

She felt something change inside of her, as if a slate covered with the bitter words of all her pent-up feelings about her mother and about Joe had suddenly been washed clean. She smiled across the table at her mother, who'd been watching Julia with a searching expression. "How's retirement so far?" Julia asked.

Her mother made a face. "Your father is driving me crazy."

Julia laughed. "Yeah? How?"

"He got too used to being the boss at the office. Now he wants to boss me around the house. I can't do one simple thing around here that he doesn't have his nose in it."

There was no venom behind the words. Her mother's eyes were twinkling, in fact; she loved her husband to pieces.

"Where is he now?" Julia asked.

"Next door helping Tony move some boxes and things down from the attic." Her mother hesitated. "They're turning the house into apartments, did you know?"

Julia felt her heart clench. "No. When?"

"Soon. Tony's been packing boxes for the last week. Sylvie was over yesterday going through her things. She said Joe and Tony are going to help her get set up with her own apartment."

"I had no idea."

"I was shocked at first," her mother confided. "That house carries a lot of memories. It'll be sad to see the Rossetti's go."

"I knew Joe had moved out. But where is Tony planning to go?" Julia hoped her mother didn't hear the fear in her voice. Where was he going? Would he be moving far away? That didn't make sense, not with the business and the television series…

"He's been looking at houses." Her mother grimaced. "He promised he'd find some good tenants. I hope so. Last thing I want is a bunch of college kids next door, partying to all hours."

"I'm sure he will," Julia replied vaguely.

"You haven't been here since…" Her mother shrugged. "Maybe you should go over there now, take one final look at the place. That might help with…things."

"Closure, you mean?"

"That's the word I was looking for. God, this menopause is making my brain foggy."

Julia stretched her hand across the table to touch her mother's. "I'm okay now, Mom. Really. I can finally talk about Joe without feeling angry or sad. I think I'm finally over that whole mess."

Her mother turned her hand over to grip Julia's tightly. "Are you sure, honey? You're not just saying that to make me feel better? I just want you to be happy. That's all I've ever wanted."

"I know." She squeezed her mother's hand. "You know what? I'm discovering that sometimes happiness can be found in the most unexpected places."

She strolled over to the Rossetti house with feelings of both trepidation and anticipation flowing in her veins. The last time she'd set foot inside the house was the day Joe had broken up with her. It had been a quiet Sunday afternoon. Both Tony and Sylvie had been out for the day. Joe had invited her to sit at the kitchen table. He'd said he had something important to tell her.

She remembered thinking it had to do with the wedding plans, that he'd changed his mind about the reception venue; they'd been going back and forth about that for days. He'd been stalling on sending the deposit.

Strange, how your whole life could change in mere seconds.

The front screen door screaked as she opened it slowly. It was a warm morning, one of those gorgeous September days that belied the approaching autumn. All of the downstairs windows were open, letting in the cleansing breeze. As she stepped into the front hall, she heard shuffling sounds coming from the stairs and her father's voice.

"I've got this end. You walk down first."

Curious, she moved to the bottom of the staircase, catching sight of Tony's backside as he stepped carefully down the stairs. He was carrying one end of an oak dresser, her father the other.

She kept quiet, not wanting to startle them. Her eyes slid downwards to admire Tony's butt and his long legs encased in a pair of old blue jeans. He was wearing a snug, light blue polo shirt that revealed his strong, corded forearms.

She moved aside as he reached the last step. Her father saw her first. He smiled. "Hey, there," he said with a huff of exertion. "Your mother said you might stop by."

Tony swiveled his head around. His face brightened. "Julia! What are you doing here?"

"My mom said you're moving out?" she blurted. She felt her cheeks redden; she'd intended to be more subtle.

"Hang on a sec," he said, slightly out of breath. He walked backwards across the hallway and into the living room, her father following. They set the dresser down with a thud.

Tony wiped his hands on his shirt and came back to her. His eyes searched her face. "Yeah, Sylvie and I are moving out. No sense in staying here any longer now that Joe is gone."

"Oh." She swallowed. Her eyes flitted briefly to her father who was observing them both with a curious expression. "This is kind of a shock. It'll be strange not seeing all of you here anymore."

To her mortification, she felt the sting of tears behind her eyes. She looked away from Tony to her father again, but she couldn't find her voice. She sent her father a look of mute appeal.

Her father cleared his throat. "I think I hear your mother calling me. You all set for now, Tony?"

"Yeah, I'm good." Tony shook her father's hand. "Thanks for helping, Tom. I'll keep you posted on the progress here."

"Do that. And let me know if you need any more

help moving things. I've got nothing but time on my hands these days."

"Will do."

The door banged shut after her father.

Tony stepped closer to Julia. "Hey. You okay?"

She couldn't meet his eyes. Her gaze darted from the hallway to the living room. There were boxes stacked on the floor, furniture pulled away from the walls, bare spots on the hardwood floor where area rugs had once been. "Why didn't you tell me you were moving?" she asked, her voice sounding a little shrill to her own ears.

"Things were put into motion just this week."

"And Sylvie's okay with this? Joe?"

He came to stand directly in front of her. He set his hands on her shoulders, prompting her to look at him. "What's wrong? Why do you look like you're about to cry?"

A lump rose in her throat. "I don't know. I guess I'm a little shocked. There've been so many changes lately..." A single tear rolled down her cheek.

"Aw, Julia. Don't do that. Don't cry."

He tugged her into his arms, hugging her tightly as he rocked back and forth. He rubbed one hand up and down her back. "I had no idea you'd react this way," he said in a husky, rough voice. "You haven't been here since May. I didn't think you were so attached to this place anymore."

"It's not the place, so much as the memories," she said into his shirt. "I guess I just took it for granted that you—that all of you—would always be here. I know that's not realistic, is it."

"No. This place is too big and empty with Joe gone and Sylvie hardly ever here. I thought about doing some renovations and making this a home for my wife and kids someday. But, I can't." His voice grew lower, darker. "Not all of those memories are good ones. You know that. It's time to start fresh."

She leaned back in his embrace so she could look at him. "Where will you go?"

"Not too far. I've been looking at some houses in the Cumberland area."

The emotion that washed through her almost had her sagging to her knees. She clutched Tony's shoulders. "That's not too far." There was no way she could conceal her relief.

Something flashed in his eyes. "You thought I was moving farther away?"

"It crossed my mind."

"You thought you'd never see me again?"

She lowered her eyelashes. Uncertainty about her feelings for this man had her adding a degree of coolness to her voice. "Not just you. All of you. You've been my second family."

He took a step back. When she stole a glance at him, his face was expressionless. His chest rose on a deep inhale. He patted her shoulder before dropping his arms to his sides. "Don't worry. We'll always be around." He waved a hand towards the stairs. "Do you want to have one last look around the place?"

Strangely, she didn't. The house already felt empty. 'No, that's okay." She tapped her forehead. "I've got all the pictures up here."

He braced his hands on his hips and leaned his weight on one leg in a casual stance. "So, what are your plans for the rest of the day?"

"Nothing. I have a rare lazy Sunday afternoon."

"Do you want to come with me to look at a

house?"

"Right now?"

"I'm meeting the realtor at one o'clock."

"In Cumberland?"

"Yeah."

"Okay."

A dimple reappeared on his cheek. "Good. I have to get cleaned up. Why don't you go visit with your mom and dad? I'll be over to get you in about twenty minutes."

Chapter Eight

"What do you think?" Tony asked as he pointed towards the gray, colonial style house situated on top of a small hill just off a quiet road.

"That's it?" Julia asked. "It's beautiful. I love the red shutters."

"Yeah. This one just came on the market. I had another place in mind, but when I saw this one..."

They drove up the long driveway. A jeep was parked outside the four car garage. A dark-haired woman who appeared to be in her forties hopped out of the vehicle. She was dressed casually in jeans and a lightweight sweater. "That's Dalia," Tony said. "She's cool. I've been working with her for a couple months now."

"So, you've been planning to move for a while."

"Yes." He switched off the ignition and gave her a warning look. "Now don't be too enthusiastic. I don't want her thinking my heart is set on this one."

She smirked. "Yes, sir."

He flashed a grin at her before getting out of the truck. Before she could open her door, he was there to do it for her. He took her hand to help her down.

The drive from Providence had only taken a half hour. During the trip, she'd shared snippets of news about her parents. She'd intentionally kept the conversation light, still feeling a little embarrassed about her reaction earlier. Still pretending that her heart hadn't skyrocketed when he'd held her in his arms and consoled her.

Tony released her hand and moved forward to greet the older woman. Then he introduced Julia. "This is my friend, Julia. Thought I'd get her perspective."

Dalia greeted Julia warmly. "It's good to have a woman's input when you're looking at a family home." She waved a hand towards the surrounding scenery. "This is a great area. You feel like you're in the country, but it's still convenient to the shops and schools. The plot is just slightly over two acres. So you have your privacy, too."

She led them alongside the garage towards the front entrance, continuing her spiel about the neighborhood.

Julia admired the fanned window above the front door. There was a brass knocker on the door in the shape of an eagle.

Dalia opened the lock box to retrieve the house key. "The current owners are retiring to Florida. This has been their family home for forty years. They did a major remodel two years ago."

The woman continued to tout the home's features as Tony and Julia stepped into the wide entranceway. Julia's eyes were drawn to the open staircase that led to the second floor. The floors were a beautiful hardwood in a rich, dark color.

"Cherry wood," Tony said, watching her appraisal.

"Yes," Dalia said. "You have hardwood floors throughout the house, tile in the bathrooms and utility room. Over here is the front room and dining room."

As the woman led them down the hallway, Tony rested his palm in the small of Julia's back. "It's very spacious, isn't it," he commented.

"Yes. I like all the windows. It makes it feel light and welcoming."

"The kitchen is just through here," Dalia called over her shoulder. "It has all the upgrades. Stainless steel appliances, granite countertops. There's even a brick oven."

Tony's warm touch guided Julia into the kitchen. "This is nice," he said. He looked at her. "Don't you think?"

"Yes. Plenty of counter space, but the room isn't so big as to be overwhelming."

"Exactly," Dalia said. She opened a glass-paneled door. "And this leads out to the backyard. The deck is new. There's even a fire pit."

Tony and Julia followed her outside onto a wide back deck with built-in benches along the perimeter. Julia's attention was caught by the view in the distance. "Look, Tony! There's a creek and a pond down there." She turned her face up to his.

He smiled at her, his eyes alight. "So there is."

"That land can never be built on," Dalia said. "Isn't that wonderful?"

Julia moved towards the railing. "What a great place for kids to play. They could ice skate there in the winter."

"How many bedrooms are there?" she heard Tony ask behind her.

"Four, including the master bedroom. Shall we go upstairs?"

Tony's hand settled on Julia's back again as they followed Dalia up the stairs.

The older woman showed them the guest en suite bedroom and two smaller bedrooms before she opened the door to the master bedroom. "From what I understand, there were five bedrooms originally, but the owners took down the wall to expand this room. Isn't it lovely?"

Julia's gaze latched onto the king-size bed situated in the far corner near a small fireplace. A vision suddenly flashed through her mind of her and Tony in this room, in that bed. She blinked in shock. She quickly glanced away, forcing her attention on Dalia as the other woman showed them the walk-in closet and then directed them to the bathroom.

"I just love this Jacuzzi tub," the older woman gushed. "Wouldn't it be nice to take your bath here and look out at the view?" She pointed to the window over the bath.

"As long as no one is looking in," Tony said with a chuckle. "Not sure I want the neighbors looking at my wife in all her naked glory. I'd have to put a privacy screen on that."

Wife? Julia gave him a sideways glance, but his eyes were on Dalia as she pointed out the walk-in shower and brushed chrome fittings. He asked the woman a few questions about the remodel and then mentioned he'd like to bring his own crew in to do an appraisal.

"Of course," Dalia said enthusiastically, sensing a sale in the making. "Whatever you need to do."

"Do you mind letting Julia and I take another look around?" he asked.

"Not at all. I'll go wait outside."

After she'd left the room, he turned back to Julia.

His expression held a curious mix of eagerness and uncertainty. "Well? What do you think?"

She glanced away from him as she moved back into the bedroom. She gave a shrug. "I think your wife will like it," she said, glad to hear the casualness in her tone.

"You think?"

"Yes. That bathroom is great. And she's going to love the walk-in closet."

"And this bedroom?" His voice was low.

"It's very spacious."

"I like the fireplace." He'd moved closer behind her. She felt his breath on the back of her neck, the heat of his body seeping through her blouse. "It'll be nice to snuggle in bed with her on a chilly winter night, the fire snapping and crackling."

"Mm, yes. Cozy."

"Do you think she'll like the kitchen?"

"It has everything she'll need."

"I wonder if three bedrooms will be enough."

"Why?"

"She told me she wants a big family."

Her heart constricted. She spun on her heel and walked hurriedly towards the hallway without looking at him. "I guess you could always build bunk beds," she tossed flippantly over her shoulder.

"Now there's an idea."

His soft laughter followed her down the stairs. She headed for the kitchen. Once there, she placed her palms on the cool granite counter on the center island. She felt like rivers of fire were flowing through her veins. She was angry. She was sad. She felt...foolish. Why had she thought Tony was interested in her? She'd misread him completely.

"Something wrong?" he asked with insouciance as he came to stand beside her.

She bit her inner cheek. She shook her head. "Not at all," she said, managing to sound cool and collected. "This really is a great house, Tony. A perfect place to raise a family." She turned towards him, a placid smile on her face. "Who's the lucky lady?"

He grinned. "I haven't asked her yet."

"Is she the one you mentioned last Saturday?"

"Yes."

"But you won't tell me her name."

"I don't want to jinx it. It's still early days yet."

She took a deep breath. "Well," she said brightly. "I wish you the best of luck with that. I look forward to meeting her someday."

"Yeah. I look forward to that, too."

She narrowed her eyes at his nonchalant expression. "You're not planning on buying this place without her seeing it first, are you?"

He shrugged. "You like it. That's enough of a woman's perspective for me."

"Her tastes might be completely different from mine. Maybe she wants to live in the city."

He shook his head. "No. I think she'll be ready for a change of scenery." He nodded towards the front hallway. "Ready to go?"

For the next two weeks, Julia put all her focus on her work. Or, at least she tried to. She had a small corporate function during the last week of September that had gone off without a hitch. And her plans for Audrey's party were coming along with just over two weeks to go before the event. She fielded calls from the woman on an almost daily basis. Audrey had decided to expand the event to include an open house for the public earlier in the day, concluding with the private party in the evening.

"We might as well, given all the work you and Tony are putting into the décor," Audrey insisted. "How's he doing, by the way? I haven't seen him since that day you both visited the factory."

"Oh, fine."

"He *is* planning to come to the party, right?"

"As far as I know."

"Now Julia, I know you'll have to work setting up this event, but once that's all done, you'll be able to relax and enjoy yourself, won't you?"

Ah, the naiveté of those unfamiliar with the world of event management; they never seemed to notice all the work that was happening behind the scenes. "I'm not sure," Julia hedged. "I have to keep an eye on the caterers, the alcohol consumption, make sure the band comes back from their break, be available if there are any snafus, etcetera..."

"Don't you have assistants for that?"

"Yes. I have two. They'll be just as busy as me."

"Sylvie had a great idea. Why don't you hire a couple of interns from Johnson and Wales? They have an excellent event management program there."

"There's a thought."

"Do it. I insist that you enjoy my party."

"Not sure I can find interns with just two weeks' notice."

"Don't you worry about it. I'll have Sylvie make some phone calls."

The woman was a steamroller. "Okay. I'm sorry. I have to hang up now. My other line is ringing."

Julia rubbed her forehead as she punched the button on her desk phone to answer the second line. "Hello?"

"How's everything going?"

"Tony. What's up?" She put him on speaker phone so she could rub her temples.

"Now there's a warm greeting for someone you haven't seen in two weeks."

"I've been busy. You know that. How's the rigging coming along?"

"That's one reason I called. It's all done. I got a call from the fabric supplier. Everything should be ready by Monday. And I'll have Audrey's display cases ready by the end of next week."

"Good. What's the other reason for your call?"

"What's the matter, Jules? You sound stressed."

"Because I *am* stressed. Audrey's been calling me every day. She's changed her mind at least three times about which appetizers she likes best. She needed to listen to demos from every band I've put in front of her, plus she's turned this into an all-day event. Did you know that?"

"Yeah. She called me earlier. I'm surprised you're not taking this all in stride. You must've had clients who are worse than she is."

Oh, yes she had. But that was Before Tony—that serene time in her life when her every waking thought hadn't been occupied with him. It was all she could do to focus on simple daily tasks.

She'd never felt this way when she'd been with Joe. Wedding plans had consumed her thoughts more than anything else. Had she thought about the way Joe smiled? The way his eyes crinkled at the corners, or his cheek dimpled, or the way his white teeth flashed? Had she lain awake late into the night imagining his dark, bourbon voice whispering in her ear or the touch of his fingers against her skin?

No. Never. And Joe didn't have a dimple in his cheek. And his voice hadn't made her think of bourbon either.

Tony's did. Damn him.

She gave a heavy sigh. "Why are you calling again?"

"Fabric. In on Monday. And, once we're all set up, I'd like you to be my date for the evening."

Julia practically flew out of her chair. She started to pace. "Your *date*? What about that woman you're seeing?"

"She'll, uh, be out of town. She won't mind me taking my friend to a party."

"She knows about me?"

"Of course. I explained to her what good friends you and I are."

Good friends.

"I can't," Julia bit out. "I'll be working the event. I won't have time to hang out with you. Bring another friend. Call up one of the girls in your little black book. I'm sure there are plenty in there."

"Can't. I threw that out months ago."

"Seriously?"

"Seriously. Once I realized this girl was the one for me, all of those other girls became so much proverbial dust in the wind."

"I don't believe you."

"Believe it, sugar. I'm a new man. I've put aside my wicked ways." He gave a soft, sultry chuckle. "Well, not *all* of them. Gotta keep something for my wife to look forward to on our wedding night."

"You haven't slept with her yet?"

"Now that's a very personal question. But, as a matter of fact, I haven't. Keeping things on a low simmer with her, letting the anticipation build. By our wedding night, she's going to be climbing all over me."

"I don't want to listen to this anymore. I'm hanging up." She reached for the handset.

"Wait. Listen." His voice turned serious. "You know Willa and Joe are going to be there. I want to be by your side for moral support. Don't you agree?"

Honestly, she hadn't given Joe and Willa much thought lately. *One* good thing was coming out of her preoccupation with Tony in any case. "I'm a big girl. I can handle it."

"You won't need to hold my hand?"

"No."

"Good girl."

"I'm not a dog."

"Speaking of dogs, which breed do you like best? Labradors or Golden Retrievers?"

"Why?"

"I've always wanted a dog. Now that I've bought a house of my own, I want to get a dog."

"You bought that house?"

"Yep. The offer was accepted last week. Congratulate me."

Her heart sank at the thought of him living in that beautiful house with his mysterious new bride, their ever-growing brood of children and a big, tail-wagging, slobbery-tongued dog. "Congratulations."

"Thank you. So, what kind of dog should I get?"

"I don't know! Why don't you ask your girlfriend?"

She hung up on him.

On the morning of Audrey's event, the clouds rolled in, dark and threatening. Julia kept one eye on the sky and one eye on her car's speedometer as she hightailed it over to Audrey's factory in Pawtucket. She was supposed to meet Tony and his crew at nine o'clock, and it was already half past the hour.

When she pulled into the parking lot, gravel flying in her wake, Tony was there to greet her. He was leaning against one of the Rossetti Construction pickup trucks, arms folded across his chest. He was wearing jeans and a long-sleeved plaid work shirt rolled up to the elbows. She tried to ignore the way his broad shoulders and chest narrowed down to his trim waist and muscular thighs. She wasn't very successful.

He strode over and opened her door.

"Were you speeding?"

"Yes."

"Bad girl."

She scowled at him. "Practicing for when you get your dog?"

He grinned. He held out his hand to help her out.

She ignored it. "Where's the rest of your crew?"

"Inside. They already have most of the rigging installed."

Her mood lightened. "Really? That's great. What time did you all get here?"

"Eight o'clock."

Julia grabbed her shoulder bag and a box of supplies from the passenger seat. Joe held out his arms to take the box.

"My staff is arriving at ten" she said. "If we stay on

schedule, we should have everything ready to go before the open house starts at noon." She looked up at the sky. "God, I hope it doesn't rain."

He followed her glance. "Doesn't look promising."

She stepped out of the car and nudged the door closed with one hip. "Do you think people will still come?"

"Are you kidding? Free food? Free tours and demos? Raffle prizes? Live music? Not to mention free parking? They'll show. Don't worry about it."

They walked side by side towards the building entrance. "I hope you're right."

"You need to have more confidence in me, Julia. There'll come a day when you're just going to have to trust me implicitly. No questions asked."

"Blind faith?"

"Yes."

"Hmm."

Looking up at him, she caught the remnants of a mysterious smile before his expression smoothed over.

Inside the huge factory building, Tony's crew was affixing the last panel to the ceiling. The long curtains of gauzy white material were hung throughout the room, creating different "rooms" to break up the expansive floor space. As she hadn't been able to find the exact shades of blue material to achieve her ocean theme, Julia had decided to use gobos instead. The pieces of glass, when affixed to the front of the small spotlights scattered throughout the room, would project intricate, wavy patterns in blue, aqua and green tones against the white fabric. A bubble machine would add to the illusion of an underwater world.

A stage had been set up in one section. The band would be arriving at eleven to set up their equipment and do a sound check. She'd hired two bands—one for the day and one for the evening—that specialized in reggae music. A steel drum trio would entertain guests with calypso music when the bands were taking their break.

The catering company would be arriving at ten-thirty. She'd kept the food simple for the open house: fish tacos, shrimp and vegetable skewers and sliders. One of her assistants had come up with the idea to hand out boxes of goldfish crackers for the children to nibble on—and adults, too, if they wanted.

The evening offerings would be more substantial, including various food stations offering a variety of fish and meat options as well as decadent desserts. Beer and wine would be served. Martinis poured in glasses with blue lights in the stems would also be offered.

In spite of all the stress of the previous three weeks, everything seemed to be coming together perfectly. As much as she loathed admitting at this point, Julia was grateful to Tony for helping with the panels. The event would not have had such an amazing visual impact without them.

He set her supply box on a nearby table and turned towards her. "Is there anything else you need?"

She shook her head. "I think I'm all set for now." Impulsively, she moved closer to him and gave him a hug. "Thanks for all your help, Tony. I really do appreciate it."

His arms wrapped around her waist. He held her closer. "My pleasure."

She would've moved away, but his arms tightened.

"How are you doing, Jules?" he asked softly. "Are you really up for seeing them tonight?"

"Yes," she answered, just as softly. She inhaled his scent—a hint of spice and the clean, male fragrance that was uniquely Tony. "I can handle it."

"What will you say to them?"

"Hello?"

His chest rumbled with laughter. "That's all?"

"I don't know. I'll play it by ear."

"Joe said he's looking forward to seeing you. I don't think he's been able to completely settle in to his new life with Willa yet. Not until he's finally convinced that you're okay."

She leaned back in his arms to look at his face. "What is he looking for? Absolution?"

"No. Not that." He paused. "Once, when I was around thirteen, I remember waking up one night to see him standing in my bedroom doorway watching me. I asked him what he was doing. He said he was just checking to make sure I was okay. When I was in high school and staying out late, he was always there waiting for me to come home, no matter how late it was. It was the same for Sylvie. He told her once that he couldn't go to sleep each night until he was sure we were both home, tucked in bed, safe and sound."

"What are you trying to say?"

"I think he's just looking for peace of mind, Julia. You're his family, too. He just wants to make sure you're safe and sound."

Julia's body sighed against his. If Joe had been there at that very moment she would have told him that, right now, in Tony's arms, she was feeling very safe and sound indeed.

Chapter Nine

The party was in full swing. Everything seemed to be running without a hitch. Her two assistants plus the college intern she'd brought on board were doing a fantastic job. Best of all, it wasn't raining. Storm clouds still threatened, but not a drop of rain had fallen yet.

Julia allowed herself to relax as she stood behind one of the curtain panels and watched the party guests mix and mingle. A few people were on the small dance floor, gyrating to the reggae beat. Others were strolling amidst the display cases that showcased Audrey's latest designs.

"This day has been a *huge* success, Julia. Everything looks amazing."

Julia pivoted around to find Audrey standing behind her. The woman was beaming.

"Thank you," Julia said with a smile. "So far, so good."

Audrey scanned the room. "I haven't seen Tony. Is he around?"

"No. He had to leave just before noon. There was some kind of emergency at one of the job sites."

Audrey pursed her lips. "That doesn't sound good. I hope everything is okay."

"Me, too."

"That must be why Joe hasn't arrived yet either." Then Audrey pointed over Julia's shoulder. "Hold on. Look who just showed up."

Julia turned towards the main entrance to see Joe and Willa standing just inside the door. Joe's expression was somber. Willa was clinging tightly to his hand and gazing up at him with a worried look.

The first emotion that took hold of Julia was fear. *Tony*. Something had happened to Tony. Without a second thought, she walked quickly towards the couple. "Is everything okay?" she asked in a breathless rush, her eyes fastened on Joe's stern face.

He'd been looking around the room. He turned his head, startled. "Julia."

"Is everything okay?" she asked again. "Is Tony okay?"

He touched her arm in a reassuring gesture. "Tony's fine. Sorry if I look a little stressed. There was an accident this morning at one of the job sites. A section of scaffolding collapsed. Two of our employees were sent to the hospital."

Julia released a deep breath. "Oh, no. I'm sorry to hear that. Will they be all right?"

"Yeah. One has a broken leg. The other guy has a concussion. They're keeping him at the hospital overnight. Tony's been there for most of the afternoon. But he should be here soon."

Julia became aware of Audrey and Collette hovering. Collette moved forward. "What a relief," she said. "The look on both your faces when you first walked in gave me a scare."

"Sorry, Collette," Willa said. She gave Julia a direct, guileless look. "It's not just the accident that has us both frazzled. I've been nervous about seeing Julia."

Julia met the younger woman's eyes. Truthfully, she'd never been angry with Willa, just angry with the situation. And something else had shifted inside of her when she first saw them at the door. When she thought that something bad had happened to Tony, it made her finally realize that some things in life were more important than others. Holding grudges seemed pretty pointless.

Observing the lingering worry in Willa's eyes, Julia allowed her expression to soften. "No need to be nervous," she said. "We're all adults. I'm over it. I really am."

Joe glanced around them; they were gathering a curious audience. He gave Julia a questioning look. "I'm glad to hear that. Is there somewhere a little more private where we can talk? Just the three of us?"

"Use my office," Audrey suggested. She pointed towards a far corner of the factory floor.

Julia walked alongside Joe and Willa towards the small room. Once inside, Joe closed the window blinds. Then he turned to Julia. "Did you really mean what you said? That you're over it?"

"Yes."

His shoulders relaxed. "Good. I know I said it over and over that day, but I said a lot of things that might have been lost in all the emotion. I'm sorry I hurt you, Jules. That's the last thing I wanted."

Julia straightened her shoulders. "I know that. And I heard you. You and your brother need to stop treating me like I'm made of glass. What hurts me now is the thought that you were willing to sacrifice your own happiness just to make me happy. In the end, I felt like you felt *obligated* to marry me because of all the support I gave you and your family over the years. That's not right."

"No, it's not," he agreed. "I was too stubborn to realize that at the time. I *do* love you, Julia. You were my best friend."

"I know."

"Will we be able to return to that?"

"Yes." She nodded at Willa who was standing close to his side. "But I won't be your best friend, Joe. Willa's your best friend now."

He looked at Willa. His eyes softened. "Yes. She is."

Julia's heart constricted at the way they were looking at each other. Envy spiraled through her blood. Would a man ever look at *her* that way? Would she ever have that same connection?

It was Willa who broke eye contact first. She returned her attention to Julia and smiled shyly. "I'm glad you and Joe were able to talk tonight. He's been so worried about you. He hasn't been sleeping well."

Joe's cheeks turned ruddy. "Willa."

"It's true. And when he doesn't sleep well, I don't sleep well."

Julia found the clipped, direct way the woman spoke strangely endearing. She could see how Willa could bring out the protective side of Joe. Feeling suddenly like a much older sister, Julia reached out and set her hand on Willa's arm. "We can't have that." She forced lightness into her tone. "Now stop worrying. Both of you. I'm fine. I'm moving on."

"That's what Tony said," Willa confided. "He says you're ready for the next step."

"Willa."

Joe's voice held caution. He and Willa exchanged a

look. Joe looked a little hesitant when he turned back to Julia. "There's something we want to tell you. You're the first person to know."

"Oh?"

He took Willa's hand and drew it into the crook of his arm. He smiled at her and then at Julia. "We're getting married. The day after Thanksgiving."

Julia felt a tiny pain in her heart. She recognized that she didn't hurt because Joe was marrying Willa. She just missed the idea of getting married herself, all the abandoned plans for her *own* wedding day. "Congratulations," she said, glad to hear how calm and sincere her voice sounded. "But that's just five weeks away. Do you need my help with anything?"

Joe's eyebrows shot up. "You'd do that?"

"Of course. I'm not a wedding planner. But I have all the connections. I could hook you up with some of my vendors. Will there be a reception?"

He shook his head. "No. It's going to be a very small, intimate ceremony. We're getting married at the Conimicut house. There won't be more than a dozen people there."

"Wow, that *is* small." And then Julia nearly bit her tongue. Tony had told her that Willa didn't have any family; of course the guest list would be small. She gave Willa a warm smile. "But sometimes those can be the best kind of weddings. No fuss. It's so much more relaxing."

Willa's return smile was sweet. "We were going to wait until February," she said. "I thought it would be fun to get married on Valentine's Day. But..."

She and Joe exchanged another speaking look.

There was a mix of apprehension and pride on Joe's face when he looked at Julia. "The fact is...

Willa is going to have a baby."

Julia slapped her hand across her mouth. Her heartbeat clamored in her ears. It took every ounce of willpower she had to pretend this news didn't upset her. "Oh. Oh! That's wonderful." She moved closer to hug Willa, then Joe. "I'm so happy for you both," she said in a shaky voice. She patted Joe's back before moving away. "I always thought Joe would make a great father," she said to Willa.

Willa took Julia's hand and pressed it. "We want you to come to the wedding," she said. "You're family. You always will be."

Julia sat alone in Audrey's office. She'd told Joe and Willa that she needed to take a break for a few minutes, that her feet were killing her after standing on them all day. They'd believed her. After one more round of hugs, the couple had left her alone.

She wasn't upset that they were getting married. That had already been a given. But the fact that Willa was pregnant, that she was going to have Joe's baby… A year from now, that might have been Julia. *She* might have been the one expecting a child. That had been the plan. She and Joe had talked about starting a family right away. She dreamed of having children of her own.

Time was running out. The prospects of finding a good and decent man to marry and start a family with within the next year or two were slim. She was thirty-three years old. This thing, this infatuation—if that's what it was—with Tony wasn't going to lead anywhere. There wasn't any point in even imagining the possibility of starting something with him. He already had his future wife in his sights.

There was no one. She was all alone.

"Julia, what are you doing in here?"

Tony stood in the doorway, dark and handsome in a charcoal suit and tie. He took one look at her face and quickly shut the door behind him. She heard the snick of the door lock.

She took several gulping breaths, striving to stay cool and collected. It was no use. All her emotions rose to the surface. To her complete mortification, she burst into tears. They weren't pretty tears. They were loud and ugly.

In two strides Tony was at her side. He lifted her into his arms and then sat down in Audrey's executive chair, holding Julia on his lap. He curved one arm around her waist, the other around her shoulders. He cupped her head with his big hand and cradled her against his firm chest.

"What is it? Is it Joe? Did he say something to hurt you?"

She shook her head, her sobs escalating.

"What is it, honey? Don't cry. You know I don't like to see you cry." He smoothed his hand over her hair.

"They... They're having a b-baby!"

"What? Who?"

"J-Joe and Willa. She's h-having his baby."

"Wow. That's great! I'm going to be an uncle."

"And they're getting m-married. Next month."

He stiffened. "And that upsets you?"

"No." She shook her head in swift denial. "No. I'm over him. I'm m-moving on. I told them that."

His body relaxed. "Then why are you so upset?"

"Because *I* want that," she wailed. "I want a man who will l-look at me the way Joe looks at her. And I want to have a baby."

"Who says you won't?"

"I'm *old*!" The word came out in three wailing syllables.

Tony gave a scoffing laugh. "You're not old."

"I'm thirty-three! I only have a few years left to start a family. And I don't even have a b-boyfriend!"

"True."

She fisted one hand in his suit jacket. "Do you *know* how long it takes to find a decent boyfriend, to decide whether or not he's compatible? If he's marriage material? It could take years! I don't have time for all that."

"I don't know about that," he said reasonably. What if you fall in love with a guy at first sight? He could be right here in this building tonight. You could marry him next week if you wanted to."

"Yeah, right. Love at first sight only happens in books and movies."

"It happened with Joe and Willa."

She gave a hiccupping sob. "Don't be cruel."

He was quiet for a few minutes as he rubbed her back in soothing circles. Julia's tears gradually diminished. Her body stopped shaking. She relaxed against him. She flattened her hand against his chest, suddenly very aware of his furnace-like heat beneath his shirt, very conscious of his strength and masculinity.

He leaned forward in the chair and yanked some tissues from the box on Audrey's desk. He wiped Julia's cheeks and nose. After tossing the damp tissues in the wastebasket, he placed his warm, calloused palm against her cheek, brushed his thumb gently along her cheekbone. "Tell me, Julia," he asked eventually, his chest rumbling beneath her ear. "What kind of man is your ideal? Maybe I can find him for you."

"He has to be good."

"Good? You mean good in bed?" His voice was teasing.

She poked him in the ribs. "Don't be an ass. I mean good. He has to be a man of integrity and honor."

"Ah. Those are excellent qualities. But you should still want a guy who's also good in bed. What else?"

"He has to be smart."

"True. You don't want to marry an idiot."

She thought some more. "And vulnerable. I like a man who's strong but isn't afraid to show his softer side. A man who can admit he's not always right."

"Well, that pretty much eliminates all the guys on my construction crew."

She gave a soft huff of laughter. "He needs to want a family."

"A big family, right?"

"Yes. He'll need to be a good father and provider."

"You haven't mentioned looks. What does your ideal man look like? Is he tall, dark and handsome?"

"Maybe. Maybe not. If he fits all the criteria, and the chemistry is there, he could be cross-eyed and bald for all I care."

Tony chuckled. "Aha. I know just the man for you then."

"*Sure* you do."

"I do. I can introduce you to him tomorrow if you want. He's an old college friend of mine."

She played with a button on his white dress shirt.

"So…he's your age."

"You're not open to marrying a younger man?"

She had never considered it *Before Tony*. "It depends on how young he is. And how mature."

"What's the biggest age difference you'd accept?"

"I don't know. Seven years, maybe?"

"Hmm. On second thought, my friend is probably too immature for you. He spends most of his weekends watching football."

"Ugh. No thanks."

As they talked, they snuggled closer and closer together. His fingers gently squeezed her hip, the fingers of his other hand sifted slowly through her hair. She had one hand pressed flat against his chest; the other had gradually slid upwards until it was curved around his neck. Her fingers played with the soft hair at his nape.

"Julia."

"Hmm?"

"*I'm* a man of honor and integrity. I like to think so anyway."

"Yes, you are."

"I'm pretty smart, too."

"Yes."

"And I can be vulnerable. You've certainly witnessed that."

Her pulse raced.

"I'd like a big family, too," he continued. "I know I'll be a good father."

"Yes. She'd be a fool not to marry you. You *do* have all the essential qualities most women find appealing."

"She?"

"That girl you've been talking about. The one you

bought that house for."

He brought his hands to her face. His touch compelled her to look up at him. His luminous eyes pierced her heart. "Julia. That girl I've been talking about? Baby, it's you."

And he lowered his mouth to hers and kissed her.

The room started to spin. Julia slammed her eyes shut. She gasped against his mouth, in both shock and excitement, and the kiss went from soft and tender to hard and hungry in a heartbeat. Through the clamor thundering inside of her head she heard Tony groan, the sound emanating from deep in his chest as he brought her chest flush against his. He lightly bit her lower lip before sliding his tongue between her parted lips and entwining it with hers in an erotic dance. One hand grasped the nape of her neck, fingers threading into her hair as he angled her head to allow his tongue to plunge deeper into her mouth. His kiss was sweet and rough and hot. His lips were pliant and smooth.

He skimmed his other hand down her arm, his thumb grazing the side of her breast. She quivered and his touch became bolder. He cupped her breast and squeezed. His thumb circled her taut nipple. She pushed into his questing hand and made eager sounds in her throat. She writhed in his lap. She felt the rigid length of his arousal beneath her bottom. She pressed down on it.

He groaned again. He tore his mouth from hers, catching his breath. He kissed her cheek, dragged his mouth up to her ear. He nibbled on her earlobe. "Julia. *Julia.* You taste so good. Just like I've always imagined."

She suddenly had a visual of him at thirteen, jerking off in his bed while he thought of her. She froze for a second and then pulled away from his kisses. "Oh, my God. What are we *doing?*"

His face was ruddy, his skin taut across his cheekbones. His chest rose and fell rapidly with his panting breaths. "What? What's the problem?"

"You're Tony!"

His eyebrows lowered. "And?"

"And I used to babysit you!" she wailed. "And I've slept with your *brother!*"

His glower grew darker. "Both facts that I have managed to push out of my mind completely."

"I haven't." She shoved against his chest, trying to break free from his firm hold. He wouldn't let her.

"Don't tell me you don't feel this attraction between us," he said, his voice gruff.

She swallowed, averting her eyes from his piercing gaze. "I do. That doesn't mean it's right."

He cupped her jaw, bringing her eyes back to his. "Why not? You're single. I'm single. You know me better than anyone else. And I know *you.*"

"I'm in a vulnerable place," she said, her tone pleading. "I miss being held and kissed by a man. That's all this is."

His fingers pressed into her jaw. "Bullshit."

She smoothed a hand down his chest in a placating gesture. "Don't you see? The worst thing I could do is allow this to happen. I'd just be using you to feel desirable again. That's not fair to you."

He didn't relax his grip. "I think you're just lying to yourself. You're afraid."

"Yes," she admitted. "I am. There've been so many changes in my life in the last six months. I don't want *us* to change. I like having you as my friend."

"And I'll keep being your friend, Julia. But I want

more. I want you. Do you feel how much I want you?" He ground his hips against her bottom.

"Oh, my God."

He captured her mouth with his again. Her resistance was futile. She collapsed against him, eagerly lifting her face to his for more.

God, he was a good kisser. He took total control. There was no hesitation in his touch, no concessions for her softer femininity. He sucked her tongue into his mouth, tangling his tongue with hers in slick, wet duel as his hands played with her breasts. She felt a tugging on her blouse as he swiftly undid the buttons. Then he was unfastening her bra. He took possession of her naked, swollen breasts, cupping, squeezing. He took a nipple between thumb and finger and pinched gently.

She moaned.

He released her mouth. His tongue licked hungrily down her neck. She arched her back, using the armrest for support as she offered her breasts to his seeking mouth. Her body was melting. Melting. She felt delicious quivers of delight shooting up and down her spine.

What was happening to her? She'd never felt this way before. So hot. So possessed.

"Sweet. So sweet," Tony whispered against her skin. He drew a nipple into his mouth, scraped and soothed with his tongue.

She felt a fierce clenching between her legs. She squirmed in his lap, lifting her hips in a silent plea.

His hand cupped her there through her skirt. His probing fingers and thumb found her pleasure spots with ease. He pressed down. "Do you see how much you want me, Julia?" His dark, sultry voice poured over her. "Tell me now that you don't want this."

Her blood was pounding wildly in her ears. "I do. I *do* want it." God, she sounded drugged, delirious; she almost didn't recognize her own voice. Shock rippled through her. She opened her eyes, her blurry vision gradually clearing as she stared at his passion-dark face. She battled with desire and rational thought. This was happening too fast. She was losing all control. She wasn't used to that.

She grabbed his wrist, forcing him to hold still. "Stop."

He froze. "Why? Why are you fighting this?"

"This is just sex!"

His breath hissed between his teeth. "It's more than that."

"Stop touching me."

"I can't."

She surged upright and shoved herself away from him. "Stop it, Tony. I'm serious."

He let her go.

She slid off his lap and stood on shaky legs. Her fingers fumbled as she set her bra and blouse to rights. She avoided his gaze.

"Talk to me, Julia."

She took a bracing breath. "You're moving too fast. This is all happening too fast."

"What's the point in taking it slow?" he reasoned, his voice low, almost calm. He captured her hand, persuading her to look at him. His eyes gleamed with that heart-tugging inner light that only he seemed to possess. "The truth is, I'm in love with you. I love you and I'm *in* love with you. Do you get that? I think I always have been."

While her heart sang at his confession, her

thoughts remained clouded. "That's impossible."

His grip on her hand tightened. "It's true. I was only just beginning to realize how I really felt about you around the same time you and Joe broke up."

She narrowed her eyes at him. "Would you have told me this if Joe and I were still engaged?"

"Yes." His tone was firm, assured. "Yes, I would have. You probably think that's an easy thing for me to say in hindsight. But it's true."

"I wouldn't have left him."

His gaze narrowed with irritation. "That's immaterial. He already had doubts about the engagement before he met Willa. He told me that the day he broke up with you."

Joe had told her the same thing. But it still hurt to hear the words again. "If you really love me, why did you toy with me that way? Why did you pretend that you were in love with someone else?"

He grazed his calloused thumb against her palm. "Because I wanted to get you riled. I needed to know that the passionate girl I used to argue with was still there. You were jealous. Doesn't that tell you that you're in love with me?"

"I'm not in love with you." Her words didn't sound as adamant as she would've liked.

His features shuttered. "You can look me in the eye and say that?"

She tugged at his grip. "Stop badgering me. Just stop it. You're not being fair. You just dropped a bomb on me, and you expect me to fall into your arms, be all lovey-dovey and confess my undying devotion for you? Yes, I'm attracted to you. Yes, I'd like to have sex with you. But I don't know if it's anything more than that. I don't know if there's something deeper. I don't *know* if I'm just feeling needy and insecure. You need to give me space, Tony. I need time to process this."

His grip tightened further. "How much time?"

"I don't know!" She barely managed to not stomp her feet in a childish display of frustration. She tugged again.

This time, he let her go. He gave a heavy sigh. "Okay. All right. Maybe I am being a selfish jerk. I wasn't planning on telling you these things tonight anyway. I can give you the time and space you're asking for."

"Thank you." Her tone was prim.

He rose to his feet. His eyes burned into hers. "But don't make me wait too long, Julia."

"Or what?"

"Or I'll come after you." He reached out and brushed his knuckles against her cheek. "You're mine."

She swayed helplessly into his touch.

His deep groan was swift and urgent. He latched onto her arms and brought her against him. His mouth melded with hers. He kissed her long and deep.

They were both gasping for breath when he finally released her several minutes later. "Go," he said, sounding tortured. "Just go. Before I break my promise."

She went.

Chapter Ten

After she'd closed the door behind her, he collapsed into the desk chair, legs sprawled. He scrubbed his hands down his face before clasping them behind his head and staring blindly at the ceiling. His pulse was speeding like a runaway train; his arousal was an excruciating ache in his groin.

Had he pushed too hard? Moved too fast?

Probably.

Holding her on his lap had been his undoing. She'd been all cuddled up against him, so soft and feminine. She had fit against him perfectly. Her sweet breath had whispered against his neck and become increasingly hot and panting as his touches had grown bolder.

Oh, she had wanted him all right.

She was worried that it was just sexual attraction. How could she not understand that it was so much more than that?

He'd dropped the L word way too soon. He felt frustration and disappointment clutch at his heart. She hadn't reacted to his declaration the way he'd imagined she would. She hadn't told him that she loved him, too.

That hurt.

His erection eventually subsided. He stood up, straightened his tie, and smoothed a hand over his hair. He took a steadying breath before opening the door and returning to the party.

He kept in the background, lurking behind one of the curtain panels as he watched Julia work the room. She was wearing a flowing white blouse tucked inside a straight black skirt that ended a few inches above her knees. Black heels accentuated her sleek legs.

She must've used the restroom after she'd left him. Her long blond hair was pulled back in a slick ponytail. A fresh coat of pretty pink lipstick colored her generous mouth.

Her white teeth gleamed as she spoke with a group of guests; her amber eyes sparkled as she chatted with her staff. Her hands made graceful gestures as she gave instructions to the caterers.

She was good at her job. She carried herself with such grace and confidence. He wondered why she couldn't be as confident about acknowledging her real feelings for him.

It hadn't been easy for him to grant her the time she'd requested. The ball was in her court now. He didn't like that. He didn't like not knowing what was going on inside her head. He didn't like waiting.

He would because she'd asked him to.

But not for long.

Now that he'd had a taste of her, he ached for more. God, he'd never felt this possessive over a woman. Never felt like such a...caveman, going all alpha male on her. He wanted to claim her, mark her...

"Looks like you could use a drink."

Tony spared a brief glance at his brother who had

come to stand beside him. He took the bottle of beer Joe extended towards him. He guzzled half the cold liquid down then swiped at his mouth with the back of his hand.

"I'd ask what's bothering you, but, based on where your eyes have been these last ten minutes, I think I know," Joe said.

Tony watched Julia talking with Audrey and Collette. He released a frustrated sigh. "I think I might have scared her off. I think I moved too fast."

"What did you do?"

"I kissed her. Things might have gotten a little out of control. And I told her that I'm love with her."

Joe gave a low whistle. "Wow. You did move fast. How did she react?"

"She was into the kiss. Way into it. And then she panicked." He kept his gaze on Julia, hoping his brother hadn't seen him wince. "She says she needs time to process."

"Huh."

They were silent for a few moments. They drank their beer.

"She said something to me and Willa earlier," Joe confided. "She said she didn't like the way you and I have treated her like she's made of glass."

Tony frowned. "Maybe I did once. Not anymore. I've been tough with her lately. I'm not afraid to push her buttons."

"What are you going to do now?"

Tony hitched one shoulder. "Give her the time she's asking for," he admitted, unable to conceal his impatience. "But not too long."

"I'm glad I was finally able to talk with her tonight," Joe said. "She said she's over what happened between us and that she's ready to move on. I believe her."

"I do, too." He threw a glance at his brother. "Now if I can just get her to believe in me and her as a couple."

Joe clapped his hand on Tony's shoulder. "Good luck."

Five days later, Tony was attempting to do some bookwork at his office when Audrey called his cellphone. The call was just the distraction he needed from his muddled thoughts. So far, he'd kept his promise to Julia and hadn't made any attempts to contact her since the previous Friday. But his patience was wearing thin.

"Tony," she said without preamble. "We have an emergency."

He sat up in his chair. "What's wrong?"

"I was at Julia's office this morning reviewing the final invoices from the party when her friend called."

"Hannah?"

"I think that's the name she said. I was sitting in the conference room. She left her office door open. I couldn't help but overhear."

"And?"

"She and her friend are going to Las Vegas."

Tony frowned. "Okay…"

"Doesn't that bother you?"

Hell yeah, it bothered him. "She's free to go where she wants," he said with nonchalance.

"I don't think that's a good idea."

"Why?"

"It appeared to me that she's very stressed. I overheard her telling her friend that she's looking forward to letting off some steam, exploring her options."

Tony stood up from his desk and started pacing the floor. "Exploring her options?"

What the hell did *that* mean?

"That's what she said. I heard her tell her friend to book a girl's getaway weekend."

"When?"

"This weekend. I heard her say Southwest out of T.F. Green, this Friday. And they're staying at the Four Seasons."

"Huh." He balled his free hand into a fist.

"So, what are you going to do?"

"What do you expect me to do? She's entitled to have her fun. She's not glued to my hip."

"You're not worried about her hooking up with some random guy?"

He wanted to slug something. Hard.

"Stop it, Audrey. Julia's not that kind of girl."

"I don't know, Tony. These past few months have been really tough for her. And she's not thinking clearly. She was so distracted today when we were reviewing the catering numbers."

"Thanks for letting me know." His tone was brisk.

"What are you going to do?"

"That's for me to know. Thanks for calling, Audrey."

After hanging up on her he sat back down and pulled up the Southwest Airlines website on his computer screen.

Exploring her *options*?

The only option she was going to be exploring this weekend was him.

Chapter Eleven

Julia basked in the afternoon sunshine in her poolside lounge chair at the Four Seasons. Earlier in the day, she'd enjoyed a luxurious massage and a nap while Hannah had gone shopping. They'd both just had a swim in the beautiful private pool. Now they sipped the fruit smoothies they'd purchased at the cafe and talked lazily of nothing important.

The temperature was perfect, still hovering close to eighty degrees. Julia had slathered on sunscreen and wore a wide-brimmed sunhat. On a whim, she'd purchased a daring red bikini at one of the shops at Mandalay Bay next door. She'd lost all the weight she'd gained since the break-up. These last couple of weeks, she hadn't eaten much at all.

Hannah's impromptu invite to fly to Las Vegas for the weekend was proving to be the perfect balm for Julia's frazzled nerves. Away from Providence, from work, from Tony, she was able to think more clearly, to take a step back and ponder all that had happened the previous Friday night in Audrey's office and all the things Tony had said and done before that time.

Or she could choose not to think at all.

It had been early afternoon when she and Hannah had arrived the day before. After getting situated in their guest room, they'd walked up the strip to the Forum Shops at Caesars where they'd spent several hours ambling through the various stores before having an early dinner at a restaurant that specialized in Mediterranean cuisine. On the way back to their hotel, they had stopped for a while to watch the water display at the Bellagio. When they had returned to their room, they had sat and enjoyed their view of the strip for a while before Julia had tugged the curtains closed and suggested they call it a night. Hannah had made a joke about how old they were getting as she'd switched off the light between their beds. "It's only nine o'clock!"

Yawning as she spoke, Julia had reminded her friend that they'd been up since four o'clock in the morning east coast time.

They had a return flight on Monday morning. It was fortunate Julia hadn't had any events booked this weekend. She'd needed this break. She'd been to Las Vegas several times in the past for one event industry conference or another. She had no desire to see any shows or hit the casinos. The Four Seasons was a non-gaming hotel; it fit her agenda perfectly. Hannah was a shopaholic and had already planned another shopping excursion for Sunday. She hadn't been at all put out when Julia said she'd rather laze around the pool all day and maybe get another massage.

Hannah was the best.

Julia took another sip of her drink and lifted her face to the sun. "This was the best idea ever, Han. Thank you."

"You needed it."

"Yes, I did."

Hannah flopped onto her stomach. She removed

her sunhat and shook out her shoulder-length brunette hair. She turned her face towards Julia. "Has the distance from him helped to bring you to any kind of decision yet?" she asked quietly.

"I don't know."

"How much time is he giving you?"

"He didn't say. Not much." A shiver raced through Julia as she remembered the dark passion in Tony's voice when he had told her he would come after her if she took too long to think things through.

"I love how he went all dominant on you," Hannah said, clearly on the same wavelength. "I like a guy who isn't afraid to take charge."

Julia pressed her icy drink cup to her hot cheek. "Let's not talk about him right now, Han. Okay?"

"Sure, hon."

They were both quiet for a while. Then Hannah propped herself up on one elbow and gave Julia a sly grin. "Let's go dancing tonight. We haven't gone to a club in ages."

"Where do you want to go?"

"It's Vegas, baby. The sky's the limit. Let's get some suggestions from the concierge."

Julia had packed a sexy, shimmering silver club dress on the off-chance that she and Hannah would go out. She definitely had some energy and pent-up emotions to burn. "Okay."

Tony liked to dance. She felt a stir of regret over the missed opportunity to take ballroom dance classes with him.

She had so much fun when she was with him.

He made her smile. He made her laugh. He made her forget everything except the pleasure of his company.

So why was she holding back?

Because she'd had her heart broken? Her confidence in herself, in her own desirability had been bruised. Any woman in the same circumstances would feel a spark when an attractive man held her hand or touched her face or kissed her. Wouldn't she?

She thought about the way she had felt sitting on the pier with him, or walking along the beach. Just talking. How it had seemed that her world contained more vibrant color and light whenever he was near.

He knew her. Only recently had she begun to realize that he probably knew her better than Joe did. Tony probed beneath the surface. He stirred her up, pushed her buttons, got argumentative. Especially in the last month. It was as if he'd been wearing kid gloves around her all these years. Now the gloves were off.

She liked that.

He made her think beyond the perfect wedding day to the days and days after that, to the possibility of a forever with him.

Honestly, he *was* all the things she desired in a potential husband.

She did love him. She always had. But was she *in* love with him?

Was she drawn to him, in part, because of her worry that she only had a few good years left to start a family?

God, what a horrible thing that would be to wake up one day and realize she'd only used him to suit her own selfish purposes.

He wanted to marry her. He'd bought a *house* for her, for Pete's sake. It didn't get more real than that.

She didn't doubt him. She doubted herself.

This is what happens when your self-confidence gets broken, she thought. Everything was all jumbled around inside her brain. She had no problem making work decisions, no problem juggling several demanding clients at once. But it was very, very hard to make heart decisions when one's heart was still feeling bruised.

A pool attendant came by offering Evian mists for her and Hannah along with some ice waters. As Julia brought the bottle of water to her lips, she felt someone watching her. She peeked over the rim of her sunglasses, scanning the surroundings. The pool area was busy with a mix of families, couples and singles. There was a group of college guys across the way who'd ogled her and Hannah when they'd first arrived, but those guys were now occupied with a bevy of fawning college girls.

There didn't appear to be anyone looking at her. Not blatantly anyhow.

Still...

She turned to Hannah. "I think I've had enough sun for now. You?"

Hannah yawned. "Yeah. Let's go in. I'm hungry. Think I'll take a nap later. This is the life, huh?"

The club, located at the MGM, was at full capacity. The DJ was the main attraction. Most of the crowd was facing the stage, waving their arms in the air as he worked the DJ booth with consummate skill.

Electronic dance music pulsed. Multi-colored strobe lights flashed. The thump, thump, thump of the invigorating beat echoed the pounding in Julia's veins. Caught up in the energy of the crowd, she pumped her fist in the air and swiveled her hips.

She was feeling buzzed. A good buzz. She and Hannah had shared a bottle of wine at dinner. They'd each had a mojito when they'd first arrived at the club at around eleven p.m. After dancing for a couple of hours, they'd sat at the bar for a while and enjoyed another round before heading back to the dance floor. That had been at least an hour ago.

She was happy. She wasn't thinking of anything. There was just the music, the steady beat, the joy of letting go and feeling unencumbered.

Someone bumped into her from behind. A body pressed up against her. Too close.

Damn it. Some randy jerk was *not* going to spoil her mood. This had happened a few other times already tonight. Guys getting too close to her and Hannah. This one was grinding his pelvis against her bottom.

Asshole.

She spun around and glared at him.

He looked like a college guy. Clearly drunk.

"Back off," she yelled.

"Come on, sweet thing. I'm just dancing. Just having a little fun."

"I didn't give you permission to touch me."

"Can't help it. It's crowded. Someone pushed me."

As she continued to glare at him, he held up his hands in mock surrender and backed away.

She exchanged an eye roll with Hannah before returning her attention to the DJ.

A few minutes later he was at it again.

She twisted away from him. "I said back OFF!"

He pouted. "Don't be such a bitch."

Suddenly, someone grabbed the guy's shirt collar. "The lady said to back off. Touch her again and you'll regret it." The owner of that voice shoved the college guy hard. College guy reeled backwards. His belligerent expression after he caught his balance quickly evaporated into trepidation. He held up his hands in appeasement and slunk away.

Tony?

"*Tony*? What are you doing here?"

He stood directly in front of her. Close enough that she felt the warm heat radiating from his body. He didn't look pleased. "What are *you* doing here?" he asked, his tone seething.

"Dancing. Having fun." She was shouting to be heard. "Why are you here? Are you following me?"

"Yes, I am," he shouted back without a trace of apology in his tone. "Good thing, too, from the looks of it."

She glowered. "I had it under control."

"Hardly."

"You were supposed to give me time and space. Why are you here?"

He moved closer. He gently grasped her chin between thumb and forefinger and bent his head down to hers. "Keeping an eye on what belongs to me," he said close to her ear.

Heat coiled low inside her belly. She fought to suppress an exhilarating surge of desire. "I'm not a possession. I don't belong to you. I belong to myself."

Hannah moved into their space. "Tony? Wow. What are you doing here?"

His mouth compressed in a grim line. "That seems to be the question of the night." His penetrating eyes returned to Julia.

"Go away," Julia implored, dismayed by how

quickly and easily she fell under his allure.

He narrowed his gaze, scrutinizing her face. "How much have you had to drink?"

"I'm not drunk."

"You look it."

Her glower turned defiant.

He released her chin and grabbed her hand. "Let's dance."

She tugged against his firm grip. "No."

He ignored her, pulling her along as he walked towards the back of the dance floor where it was slightly less crowded and noisy. He turned around to face her, wrapped his other arm around her waist and drew her against his body. He kept her hand clasped in his and brought it up to rest on his shoulder before he released it. Now he had both arms around her waist; his hold tightened.

She shoved her hand against his shoulder. He didn't budge. "You're being mean," she fumed.

"Am I?" he said with a smirk. He grabbed her hand and brought it behind her waist keeping it clasped in his. This brought her fully against him, her breasts thrusting forward, rubbing against his chest.

His eyes skimmed downwards. A smile of blatant male appreciation tugged at his mouth as he ogled her exposed cleavage. "Nice dress."

"Pervert."

"Almost as nice as that little red bikini you were wearing by the pool earlier."

"You were *there*? You were watching me?"

"Me and every other straight guy in the vicinity. You were the sexiest woman out there." His eyes seared into hers. "Not sure I like my girl flaunting her wares to every Tom, Dick and Harry Dick in Las

Vegas. Only I should have that pleasure."

"I thought I felt someone watching me. Where were you hiding?"

"I was on the upper patio."

She still couldn't believe he was here, holding her. The buzzing in her head accelerated along with the beat of her heart. "When did you get here?"

"This morning. All the flights yesterday were sold out. What did you and your friend do last night?"

She detected a hint of worry in his voice. The little devil inside of her had her answering flippantly, "We went to see Thunder from down Under and partied with the boys until three in the morning."

He flashed a cocky grin. "Sure you did."

She tugged at the hand gripping hers behind her lower back. "You're hurting me."

His expression turned instantly contrite. He brought her hand back around, lifting it to his shoulder before releasing it. "I'm sorry, baby. Just put your arms around me. Please? Let's just dance, okay? I need to hold you. It's been too long."

Her reluctance was short-lived. He felt so good against her, so strong and virile. He was wearing a black dress shirt untucked over dark blue jeans. The top buttons of the form-fitting shirt were undone, revealing the sleek lines of his collarbone. Releasing a helpless sigh, she flattened the palm of one hand against his chest just over his heart; she wrapped the other around his neck.

He had both arms curled around her waist again. One hand glided slowly down the curve of her bottom, pressing her even closer against him.

The beat of the music was fast, but Tony's steps were much slower. As their bodies swayed, he tucked one leg in between hers and shifted in a way that had his taut thigh pressing against the apex of her legs. She gave a little gasp, unable to prevent her hips from undulating in a way that had him rubbing her right...there.

His groan was rough, fraught with need. "God, Julia. I've missed you," he said against her ear. He brushed his mouth across her temple.

"It's only been a week."

"Too long."

"A week isn't enough time. You didn't give me time."

What sounded like a growl rumbled from his chest. He drew his head back so he could look her in the eye. "This isn't the place to talk. Let's get out of here."

"I can't leave Hannah."

He released her. "Stay here," he ordered. "I'll tell her where we'll be. There's a garden area just outside the door over there. We'll come back for her and leave together, okay?"

She nodded.

He pressed a finger to her lower lip, his hooded eyes lingering there for a moment. "I'll be right back."

She watched him weave through the crowd, admiring his height and the breadth of his shoulders. He made every guy in the immediate vicinity look like an immature frat boy.

He was back within five minutes. He took her hand and led her towards a side door. "Hannah's hanging out with a group of other ladies. She says she's fine."

Her body was still thrumming with the pounding bass of the music as she and Tony stepped outside.

She gave her head a shake, trying to clear it. The air was slightly humid due to the gushing water fountains nearby. She breathed it in, trying to regain her equilibrium as Tony led her to a shadowed corner away from a group of revelers mingling near the outdoor bar.

"You look a little glassy-eyed," he said grimly when he turned to face her. He cupped her face in his hands, tipping it back as his gleaming eyes scanned her features. "Just how much have you had to drink tonight?"

"I had some wine with dinner. A couple cocktails. I'm fine, really. It's just the loud music still buzzing in my ears."

He grazed his thumbs gently across her cheekbones. "I didn't think this was your kind of thing. The club scene."

She arched one eyebrow. "Why? Because I'm too much of a princess? Mommy and Daddy's perfect girl?"

Curiosity flickered in his expression. "Is that how you see yourself?"

"Don't you? You called me a princess once and not in a nice way."

"Did I?" He traced her lips with one index finger. "I'm sorry."

She shrugged one shoulder.

"I don't think of you as a princess," he murmured. "Or perfect. Perfect is boring. I like it that you don't mind getting your hands dirty crabbing with me. I like it that you drink beer right from the bottle and belly laugh during a funny movie. I like the way you can get snippety with me. I like it when you push back." He dipped his finger between her parted lips and slowly brushed the tip across the ridges of her lower teeth. "I don't like it when you run away from me. I don't like it when I hear that you came out here to explore your options." Derision entered his voice on those last words.

She took his finger between her teeth and bit down.

He yanked his hand away. "Ow! What was that for?"

"*I* don't like it when you tell me you'll give me time to think and then you show up here like some he-man bully just one week later."

His mouth quirked. "He-man bully?"

"That's right." She slammed her hands on her hips. "And who told you I was coming here anyway?"

"Audrey. She overheard you making plans with Hannah." He scowled. "What did you mean by exploring your options?"

Julia rolled her eyes. "That snoop."

"She cares. They all recognized how I felt about you months ago."

"And she and her girlfriends have been conspiring ever since, I bet. That whole party of hers was just a way to get us working in close proximity, wasn't it."

"Possibly. I told her to back off, Jules. I don't need any help getting my girl."

Oddly, she found the arrogant tone of his voice very sexy. He was so sure of himself when it came to expressing his feelings for her. She envied his self-confidence.

It finally struck her in a deeper way what he'd done. He'd flown across the country for her. Yes, maybe it was a bit controlling and overbearing. He'd never been that way with her before that night in

Audrey's office. But she sensed the concern and uncertainty behind his words and actions. He was sure of himself, but he wasn't sure of her.

Something softened inside of her. "When Audrey heard me talking about 'exploring my options', I was talking about my agenda for this weekend. Going to the spa, sitting by the pool, you know? That's all it meant."

His features relaxed a little. "I see. And what about us? How much time do you need to realize that you love me and that we're meant to be together?"

She couldn't help but smile at his persistence. Seeing her smile, he stepped close and captured her face in his hands once more. "*Have* you had enough time?"

"You move too fast." There wasn't any censure in her voice, only bewilderment mixed with wonder. Was this really happening? Was she about to step off the ledge and let go of some of her doubts and insecurities?

He dropped a swift kiss on her forehead and then leaned his head back to look at her. There was something in his warm, piercing gaze that shot straight into her heart. "I hadn't planned to move this fast, baby. I was going to take it slow, ease you into the possibility of us. But when I held you in my arms the other night, I couldn't wait a second longer." His raspy voice grabbed her low, right between her legs. "The thing is, when you find the person you love, the one you want to spend the rest of your life with, why wait? This is *real*, Julia. I will never leave you. Do you believe me?"

"Yes," she whispered.

Pure relief and joy washed over his face. "Say it

again," he breathed.

"Yes. I believe you."

All her senses and emotions were magnified as he lowered his mouth to hers and kissed her tenderly. "Say it again," he whispered against her lips.

"Yes."

With a stifled groan he covered her mouth with his, his kiss hungry and exploring. He wrapped one arm around her waist, sweeping her against him as he bent over her. He cupped her head with his other hand, his long fingers pressing against her scalp.

She clung to him, her palms against his face, drawing him closer, inviting him to take all that he wanted. A shudder ran through him when she sucked his tongue into her mouth and teased it with her own.

She lost all sense of place and time, completely absorbed in his taste and touch. So this is what it meant when someone said their heart felt like it was about to burst. That's the only way she could describe what was happening to her.

When he gradually pulled away from her, his chest was rising and falling with the jagged tempo of his breathing. His eyes gleamed down into hers. "I love you."

She swallowed. "I love you, too."

He smiled the most beautiful smile she'd ever seen. Something clutched at her heart that felt like fear. "I'm still scared," she confessed.

"I know, baby."

"What if I'm right? What if this is just physical attraction on my part? What if you're just my rebound guy?"

His arms tightened around her. "Remember when I told you there'd come a day when you'd just have to trust me. No questions asked?"

She nodded.

"Trust this, Julia. Trust us. That's all I ask."

She took a deep breath. "Okay."

He kissed her again.

They were interrupted by a loud teasing laugh several minutes later. "Geez, you two. Get a room!"

Tony kept his arms looped around Julia's waist as they both turned their heads towards Hannah who was standing a few feet away.

She was swaying on her four-inch heels. "The music has stopped. The party's over." Her words were a little slurred.

Tony glanced at his watch. "It's just after four a.m."

"Wow," Julia breathed. "Time flies..."

He smiled at her. "I think your friend is a little drunk."

"Looks that way."

"Why don't we all go get something to eat? Get her sobered up before I take you back to the hotel."

She smiled at his thoughtfulness. "Where are you staying?"

"I'm at the Four Seasons, too." A fire blazed in his half-hooded gaze, matching the desire sizzling through her veins.

"Hmm," was all she said, but she didn't conceal the anticipation in her voice.

His eyes held impatience and promise. "Let's go."

Chapter Twelve

Two p.m. the same day

"Good afternoon, wife. Sleep well?"

Julia blinked. "Huh?"

Tony's toffee-colored eyes were warm with concern as they traveled over her face. "How do you feel?"

"Horrible." Her skull was pounding. She carefully rubbed her eyes, feeling remnants of mascara lurking in the corners. "What are you doing here?" she asked groggily.

A shadow fell across his features. He cocked his head to one side, observing her more closely. "You don't remember?"

"Remember what?"

He frowned. "This morning. Our wedding?"

She felt a knot in her chest. "Our *wedding?*"

The little dog wriggling against Tony's bare chest gave an impatient yip as if ordering Julia to get with the program.

Tony patted its head. "Shush, Max." There was a trace of impatience beneath the disbelief in his voice as he narrowed his eyes on Julia. "Are you teasing me, Julia? Are you saying that you seriously don't remember marrying me at nine o'clock this morning?"

Her stomach roiled. She clapped her hand over her mouth, tossed the bedcovers aside and lurched out of bed. She raced to the bathroom on shaky legs and fell to her knees in front of the toilet just in time.

There wasn't anything left in her stomach, and she was doing the dry heaves when she felt a hand holding back her hair and a cool, damp cloth placed against the back of her neck.

"Christ, baby. I had no idea champagne would affect you like this."

She couldn't look at him. She swiped the back of her hand across her damp mouth. She flushed the toilet. Oh, God, he'd now seen her at her absolute worst. "I'm not a champagne kind of girl. One glass is all I can tolerate."

"Then why did you insist I order a bottle with our brunch?" His tone was flabbergasted, not accusatory.

"I did?"

He rubbed her back. He sighed deeply. "You really don't remember… This is crazy."

She was suddenly very aware of her naked butt cheeks on display and the way her bustier was pushing her breasts practically to her chin. She sat on her haunches and crossed her arms across her chest. "What the hell am I wearing?"

He chuckled softly. "That was Hannah's idea. You said you liked it. I like it, too."

She folded her arms tighter. "I guess from the fact that I'm still wearing it that we didn't have sex?"

His hand stilled on her back. "No. We didn't. You crashed on me after our champagne brunch in bed." His fingers trailed gently across her naked skin above the bustier line. "Believe me, you'll remember when

I've had sex with you, baby." He pressed a kiss between her shoulder blades.

She stiffened, very aware of how grimy she looked and felt. "I want to take a shower."

"Good idea. I'll order some lunch. I want you to take some aspirin, but you need to eat something first."

"I don't think I can."

He gave her shoulder a gentle squeeze before moving towards the doorway. "You will."

As soon as he closed the door behind him, she rose to her feet and hobbled over to the sink. Her toiletry bag was hanging from a hook. She must've moved her things out of the room she'd been sharing with Hannah.

Why didn't she remember?

She brushed her teeth three times and swallowed a cup of mouthwash. She looked at her reflection in the mirror. *Agh*. Her raccoon eyes were bloodshot, her hair was sticking up all over, and she had a pillow case crease on her right cheek. She looked horrid.

She was *married*?

She fumbled with the fastenings of the bustier, carelessly ripping the lace material as she tugged it and the thong off and threw them in the corner. She wouldn't be wearing that uncomfortable, ridiculous getup again. And she'd said she liked it? More likely Hannah had said it looked fabulous.

"*Really*, Hannah?" Julia muttered.

She stepped into the glassed-in shower and turned the knob, setting the water to a tepid temperature that she hoped would help clear her foggy head.

What had happened?

She remembered leaving the MGM. Tony had

hailed a taxi. They'd gone to some twenty-four hour diner off the strip. Tony had ordered bacon and eggs and toast for her and Hannah and steak and eggs for himself.

Okay, those were pretty vivid details. Maybe if she started with the little things the rest would come back to her.

Hannah had been a little more lucid after they'd finished eating. Tony had made her drink a couple cups of coffee. Then Hannah started prying into their relationship. Were Julia and Tony an official couple now? And Julia, ever honest and open with her best friend, had confessed that she loved Tony.

Hannah had let out a loud whoop, drawing the attention of the other diners. She'd flagged down their waitress and had ordered mimosas to celebrate. Even Tony had had one. Julia remembered being happy, relaxed…nervous but also filled with growing anticipation.

Yes, she remembered feeling slightly nervous about going back to the hotel too soon. She wanted to sleep with Tony. But the less confident part of her was thinking about all the other women he'd been with. How would she compare? She hoped he wasn't expecting a sex goddess in bed. She'd never exactly considered herself to be wild and uninhibited in the sack.

So, she hadn't put up a fuss when Hannah insisted they all go into the small casino attached to the diner and test their luck at the slot machines.

"This has been your lucky day, Tony," Hannah had cajoled. "Let's see if it continues!"

Julia remembered asking Tony for a twenty. She remembered winning, the sound of bells, lights flashing. She remembered throwing her arms around Tony's neck and pressing little kisses all over his face.

"Let's get out of here," he'd murmured against her neck, his voice dark and sexy and promising sweet, delicious sin.

And it was all fuzzy after that.

When she emerged from the bathroom a while later, wrapped in one of the hotel bathrobes, Tony was sitting at the table by the window. He'd thrown on a pair of dark blue cargo shorts, but his chest was bare. He lifted a silver dome off the plate in front of him. "I ordered fruit, yogurt and some dry toast. Okay?"

"That'll work."

She tugged the lapels of the bathrobe tighter across her chest as she slid into the chair across from him. She was very aware of her nudity beneath the robe. She felt his intense eyes on her as she pretended interest in the view of the strip. It was almost the same view as the one from her and Hannah's room.

She swiveled her face to his. "Where's Hannah?"

He gave a dry shake of his head. "Still sleeping it off, I imagine. That girl is one crazy chick."

Julia looked around the room. "Where's the dog?"

"Max is taking a nap in the closet."

She looked at Tony askance. "You put him in the closet?"

He shrugged. "The concierge gave me a pet carrier to put him in and some other supplies. Good thing this is a pet-friendly hotel." An amused smile tugged at his mouth. "You were planning on sneaking him in under your wedding dress and pretending you were a shotgun bride."

Her eyebrows shot up. "I had a wedding dress?"

How could she not remember *that*? "Where is it?"

"It was a rental. I had to pay extra because you wanted to wear it back to the hotel so I could carry you over the threshold in it. I had to have it returned by one o'clock or get charged triple." Seeing her dismay, he reached across the table and squeezed her hand. "Don't worry. Hannah took pictures. You can see them later."

Julia brought her free hand to her head. "Oh, God. I need a drink."

He released her hand, picked up a spoon and wrapped her fingers around it. "No more drinks for you except for water. Eat some yogurt."

She concentrated on eating the yogurt, her thoughts and emotions churning inside of her.

Tony's calm voice brought her gaze back to his. "We only had one mimosa at the diner," he said consideringly. "You weren't drunk when we got married, Julia. Your eyes were clear and wide-open when you said your vows to me." He shook his head. "It must've been afterwards. After we rescued Max and dealt with all that. It was eleven o'clock by the time we got back here. We were both starving. You insisted on ordering that bottle of champagne to celebrate. And you didn't eat much, now that I think about it. I was way too distracted by the lovely image of you sitting next to me in bed to pay attention."

"I don't know why I did that or why you let me. The stuff goes right to my head."

His smile was tender. "Now I know why. You were nervous about our wedding night—or wedding morning in this case. You probably thought it would relax you. We finished breakfast. I had an amazing time removing your dress and your silk stockings. I was kissing you when all the sudden you passed out on me. That was that."

She felt her bottom lip wobble. "I don't remember," she whispered. And, to her dismay, a big fat tear rolled down her cheek.

Seconds later, she was on Tony's lap, cuddled close. "You'll remember, sweetheart. Once the alcohol clears, you'll remember everything. I know you will."

"What if I don't?"

"Trust me."

She curled her hand around his neck and snuggled closer. "Where were we married?"

"The Little White Wedding Chapel."

"That's where Willa's friend, Shirley, got married," she remembered.

"That's exactly what you said when the taxi drove by the place on the way back to the hotel. You yelled 'stop the car!' and we all went inside. You said you just wanted to see the place because Shirley had said some famous people got married there. Next thing I knew, you were asking one of the wedding coordinators what the process was to get married there."

"I did?"

"You did. Twenty minutes later, we were in line at the Clark County Court House to get our marriage license."

"On a Sunday?"

"They open at eight a.m. every day of the year. This *is* the wedding capital of the world."

Her brow furrowed. "So this was all *my* idea?"

It didn't make sense. She'd always imagined her wedding day as a grand affair with all of her friends and family present. Well, that had mostly been her mother's dream, but Julia had wanted it, too. Hadn't she? Oh, God, her mother was going to have a breakdown when she found out that she'd missed her only daughter's—her only child's—wedding.

"We can't tell anyone about this," she blurted. "No one can know what happened."

He stiffened. "What do you mean?"

"My mother is going to freak. You should know that. Don't you remember how devastated she was after Joe broke things off? She's been planning my wedding since the day I was born."

He was silent for a few moments. "Maybe that's why you chose to go this route instead," he suggested. "Maybe it was a form of rebellion."

She shook her head. "That doesn't make sense. I wouldn't be that cruel to my mother. She has her faults, but she's only wanted the best for me." She reared her head back and gave him a pleading look. "We can't tell anyone we're married, Tony." She steeled her voice. "In fact, we need to get an annulment right away. I just can't believe that I was ready to marry you this quickly. I don't know if I wanted to marry you at all!"

He bolted upright. His face was livid. "No way, Julia. No way in hell are we getting an annulment or a divorce. You married me fair and square, until death do us part. I've got the certificate to prove it. I'm not letting you go."

"I was drunk! I wasn't thinking clearly!"

His jaw clenched. "You were *not* drunk." He grasped her chin and brought his face close, his eyes burning into hers. "In fact, you were thinking more clearly than you probably ever have in your life. You were following your heart."

"I wouldn't do that to my mother," she insisted, her voice shrill.

"Let's leave your mother out of this," he seethed. "This is just between you and me and what we feel for each other. Do you love me?"

Her heart lodged in her throat. She nodded mutely.

He slid his hand down her neck and then wrapped his fingers around her nape. "Then why are you fighting this? Why can't you just let us *be*?"

He swallowed her faint protest with his demanding mouth. He pushed her back against his bracing arm. His other hand tugged impatiently at the belt of her bathrobe and yanked it free. She felt cool air touching her skin as the robe draped open. She gasped against his mouth as his hand took possession of her breasts.

"This is mine," he muttered against her lips. "Feel how you want me?" He rubbed the rough pad of his thumb across one nipple. "Your body doesn't lie, Julia."

"I can't," she protested feebly. "I needed more time—"

"Stop thinking," he persisted. "Just feel."

He buried his face against her arching neck, licking his fine sandpaper tongue over her thundering pulse as his hand slid down her belly and dipped between her legs.

She parted them without a second thought, lifted her hips into his touch. She felt a long finger push inside of her, his thumb stroking her clit.

She writhed and squirmed, her bottom rubbing against the hard ridge of his arousal.

He dragged his mouth to her ear, darted his

tongue inside and took a swirling lick. She nearly flew off his lap. His brief, exultant laugh sent a blast of delicious heat into her ear. "See, Julia? See how you respond to me?"

That finger between her legs pushed deeper, curled inwards and gently scraped against a swollen place inside of her she hadn't known existed. She clutched his head, rested her temple against his as she cried out in an attenuated wail. The sweet pressure inside of her built and built until the only way to relieve the tension was to convulse and scream.

He shuddered against her, the hand at the nape of her neck gripping hard. His finger continued to thrust inside of her in a rapid, relentless pursuit of the second climax that was quickly building up inside of her.

"Tony!" she cried, her voice ringing with amazement and ecstasy. She'd never known such pleasure. It was impossible to fight against it.

Tears sprang to her eyes as she came a second time, her body quivering from head to toe. She relaxed completely in his arms, surrendering to the most perfect bliss she'd ever known.

He kissed her forehead and then her closed eyes.

His finger lingered inside of her as her body clenched around it in tiny aftershocks. When she eventually stilled, he slowly removed his finger and trailed it up her torso, between her breasts, along the arch of her neck to her chin. He slipped that finger in her mouth. "Taste what I've done to you," he commanded, his rich bourbon voice pouring over her.

She obediently coiled her tongue around his finger and tasted the essence of her pleasure.

His breath was coming in staccato gasps against her cheek when he eventually withdrew his finger and rubbed it slowly along her bottom lip. "See how good it can be between us, Julia?"

Her brain was groggy. She was complete mush in his arms. Her fingers played lazily with the corded tendons at the back of his neck. "Mmm."

His husky laugh held both male pride and unsatisfied lust. Hearing it, she drowsily opened her eyes. Her heart squeezed at the stark longing written on his face. "What about you?" she asked sleepily. She slid her hand down his chest, grazed a penny-brown nipple with her finger.

He shuddered. His features grimaced as if he couldn't believe what he was about to say. "You're still hung over. You're going to take some aspirin and then we'll take a nap." His gaze softened with his promise. "I want you wide awake when I take you. When I've come inside of you, there won't be an ounce of doubt left in that head of yours about where you belong."

Chapter Thirteen

"I still can't believe you did this," Hannah muttered with a sour expression, ignoring the flight attendant who was giving safety instructions in preparation for takeoff.

Julia had only just begun to breathe normally again. She'd sagged against her seatback with relief when the airplane door had finally been shut.

Tony had been sound asleep when she'd crept out of their bed two hours earlier. Before he'd drifted off, he'd told her that he hadn't had any sleep since five a.m. the previous day; he'd been too busy chasing her.

She'd dozed in his arms for a while, still lethargic after experiencing the most mind-blowing orgasms of her life. When she had awoken to use the bathroom, Tony hadn't stirred as she'd carefully extricated herself from beneath his heavy, limp arm.

As she'd stood in front of the bathroom mirror, studying her pale, wide-eyed reflection, all of her doubts and insecurities had churned inside of her again. Her brain had still been in a fog. She still didn't remember the wedding. Then she'd made the impulsive decision to go to Hannah's room and grill her friend for the details, hoping that would give her some peace of mind.

She'd found her suitcase next to the bedroom dresser and quietly rolled it into the bathroom. She'd quickly dressed in jeans and a lightweight sweater. She didn't bother with makeup. As she'd packed her toiletries, it had dawned on her what she was really doing.

It wasn't going to be a short visit to Hannah's room. Julia wanted to leave this hotel and Las Vegas behind her as quickly as possible. As much as she loved Tony, she simply couldn't believe that she would've done something that didn't fit into her normal, good-girl behavior.

Maybe it had been a joke, a prank. But Tony would never do something like that to her. His fury when she'd insisted they get an annulment couldn't have been faked. It had to be true. She just wished she could remember!

She couldn't think straight when she was around him. That was the problem. He was just too damn sexy and aggressive. He just had to look at her with those piercing brown eyes of his and she practically swooned like a fan girl at a pop concert.

She wasn't sure she liked being that way. She'd never considered herself weak. And she didn't like feeling vulnerable. He had been too overpowering.

She needed to get away. She needed to clear her head and calm her emotions and make sure that she hadn't just made the biggest mistake of her life. She couldn't have Tony around, influencing her decisions.

As she'd tiptoed to the door, she'd heard a faint yip from inside the closet. The sound gave impetus to her motions as she'd quietly unlocked the door and slipped into the hallway.

She didn't even remember how the dog had come

into the picture!

She'd raced to Hannah's room and shaken her awake. She'd ignored her friend's entreaties and grumblings as she'd pleaded with Hannah to hurry up. Julia's rising hysteria had finally convinced Hannah to go along with the escape. She'd insisted on taking a shower first though. Julia had frantically paced the floor, dreading that Tony would be banging on the door at any minute.

Afraid that they might bump into him in the lobby, Julia had Hannah check out of their room over the phone. Then they'd taken the elevator to the meeting rooms on the second floor and from there taken an escalator to the lobby level. They'd exited out a side door to the porte cochere. As their cab had pulled away from the hotel, Julia had looked back to make sure they weren't being followed.

Hannah had been less than thrilled to learn that the only way Julia could arrange a fast exit from Las Vegas was to first take a flight to Los Angeles, then hop on a red-eye to Providence that wouldn't get them home until nine-thirty the following morning.

"I hate red-eyes," Hannah grumbled now for what felt like the hundredth time.

"At least you didn't have to pay for it," Julia shot back. "I've now maxed out my personal credit card."

"Hey, this was your choice. We could've left tomorrow morning as planned. Why you couldn't stay put and just enjoy a healthy round of hot sex with your hunky husband is beyond my comprehension."

Julia made a shushing gesture with her hand. "Don't talk so loud. I don't want everyone on this plane knowing my business. And I've gone over this with you half a dozen times already. Why isn't it sinking in?"

"Maybe because I'm still hung over?"

Julia sighed. "Then let's talk after we've both had some coffee. And don't fall asleep on me. I need you to tell me exactly what happened."

"I can't believe you don't remember."

"Well, I *don't*, okay?" Julia could hear the anguish in her voice. "That's why I will never drink champagne again."

"Lightweight." But Hannah's tone was conciliatory. She gave Julia's arm a gentle nudge. "Just let me close my eyes until they start serving beverages, okay? You woke me out of a dream of Sam licking melted Godiva chocolate off my belly. I want to try and get back into that dream again."

Forty minutes later, after they'd each downed two cups of coffee, Hannah retrieved her smartphone from her purse and opened her photos. She swiped her finger across the screen. "Here you are at the courthouse. Isn't that sweet the way you're looking up at Tony? You look so excited."

Julia studied the photo closely. She did look excited. And happy. She didn't look drunk. She had a vague recollection of a clerk explaining the paperwork to her and Tony. She remembered sharing a secret laugh with him as the clerk snapped her gum with evident boredom.

"And here we are at the lingerie shop," Hannah continued. "You asked me to take this picture so you could share it with Tony later."

Julia cringed. "Gah! Why did you let me buy that?"

Hannah gave her a suffering look. "One, your bra and panties were all sweaty after a night of shaking it on the dance floor. And, two, you wanted to wear something with a lot of buttons for Tony to undo."

A memory flashed in Julia's head. "I did say that, didn't I."

"You remember?"

"Yes." Her voice filled with relief and excitement. "I tried on a corset, too, with red ribbons. But I wasn't feeling it." She winced. "I can't believe I chose a thong, though."

Hannah smirked. "You said Tony liked to touch your ass."

Julia gave her friend a worried frown. "Han, was I drunk?"

"No." Hannah's tone was adamant. "*I* was still feeling a buzz. You guys didn't see me sneak a seven and seven when we were at that casino. But I would've gone along with this drunk or sober. You were so excited about the whole thing. When we first arrived at the chapel and were just looking around, it was like suddenly this light switched on inside of you. You looked at Tony and said, 'You're right, why wait?' I loved how confident you were. I was so impressed."

"And Tony didn't try to convince me not to do it?"

"He did say, 'Are you sure?' And you said—"

"Absolutely. I said absolutely."

"Yep. That's what you said. Then you and Tony were kissing, and the wedding coordinators were giving instructions on where to get the license. It was just a whirlwind from that point."

"Wait. Did he ask me to marry him? Or did I ask him?"

Hannah cocked her head to one side. "You know? I don't remember either one of you asking. I think it was just a given."

Julia frowned. "I don't remember the dress. Let me see the dress."

Hannah swiped to the next photo. It showed Julia standing in front of a three-way mirror. The dress was a strapless ivory satin column gown with an empire waist. There was some pretty floral lace detail on the bodice.

"Oh," Julia said softly. "That's lovely. I do remember wearing that! I remember trying on some ball gown and princess styles. But I didn't like them."

Hannah laughed. "You said you were *not* going to dress like a princess on your wedding day."

"I did!" Julia laughed, too. She felt the lightness of relief as memories came rushing into her head. Only now did she understand just how agonized she'd been that she may have had a total blackout and would never remember anything about her wedding.

"What did you wear, Han?"

"Oh, I didn't want to be in the wedding party, hon. I took the pictures, and I was your witness. I just wanted you two up there in front of the officiant. See?"

And there they were: Tony and Julia, facing each other, hands clasped, standing in front of a kind-faced, gray-haired man. She remembered walking towards Tony down the short aisle, remembered the glow in his eyes as she drew closer. She remembered looking up at him, heart in her eyes and telling him that she would take him as her wedded partner, to have and to hold...till death do us part.

She felt pinpricks of tears behind her eyes as she beamed at her friend. "Oh, Hannah. I *did* marry him."

Hannah smiled. "It was a lovely ceremony. Only

ten minutes long, but I cried. And you were crying. And Tony's eyes were shimmery, too."

Julia glanced at her naked ring finger. "We didn't exchange rings?"

"You did! It was so cute. We stopped by a grocery store on the way back from the courthouse, and Tony put two dollars in quarters in the bubble gum machine before he found a ring that you both liked. He said he'd replace it with a real one when you got back to Providence."

Hannah smiled. "We laughed when he put it on my finger."

"Here's a picture of your hands."

The ring was a plastic silver band with a big, gaudy diamond. Tony's hand rested over hers. His own ring was plastic, too, with the jewel snapped off.

Julia laughed. "That's so sweet. I wonder what happened to them?"

"They were kind of tight. He must have them."

Julia brushed a hand across her damp eyes. "Oh, Han. I remember saying 'I do' and kissing him."

"So... Why are you running away?"

"Maybe because this isn't normal for me? This isn't something I'd typically do." She gave Hannah a beseeching look. "You know me. I like having everything in order. I like feeling in control. That's one reason why I enjoy my job. I'm good at organizing things. I was good at organizing my life."

"True."

"My life was just about perfect, wasn't it? But, since May, it hasn't been. I'm afraid that I haven't been thinking rationally."

"It's tough to think rationally when you're in love."

Julia heaved a sigh. "I asked him for time. But he didn't give it to me."

"I don't know, Jules. I think you've grown too used to living in your comfort zone. I like that Tony is forcing you out of it. I *love* that he chased you all the way across the country. That is so hot." Hannah squeezed Julia's arm. "Why can't you just let yourself go and take a leap of faith? I thought you had this morning. I was so proud of you. But now you're letting all your little demons of self-doubt take control again."

"You both expected too much from me too soon." Julia shook her head. "I mean, I was just getting past the fact that he's Joe's younger brother. I needed more time to adjust. And Tony has been coming on so strong. I'm not used to that."

Hannah's tone was firm. "When you were trying on the wedding dresses, do you know what you said to me? You said one reason you loved him was because he made *you* feel stronger, more confident in yourself. What's happened to that Julia since nine o'clock this morning?"

"Too much champagne?" Julia said with a feeble attempt at humor. "Still feeling a little scared?"

"Snap out of it!"

Julia's laughter carried an underlying tenor of dread. "He's going to be so angry when he finds out that I've left."

"No doubt. He's going to be kicking down your door as soon as he gets back in town."

Julia worried her lip. "I'll call him from Los Angeles."

During their two hour layover at Los Angeles International Airport, Julia placed six calls to Tony's cellphone. All of them went straight to voicemail. On the sixth call, she finally left a message. After taking a deep breath, she said, "I'm okay. I'm on my way back to Providence. Call me."

Chapter Fourteen

There were no messages on her phone when the plane landed at T.F. Green the following morning. After Hannah dropped her off, Julia swung by the office before heading up to her apartment. Her two assistants were surprised to see her, not expecting her back until Tuesday. She asked them if there'd been any calls from Tony Rossetti, but the answer was no. Too anxious to sleep, she took a quick shower and donned a fresh outfit before returning to the office and diving into a stack of invoices in a vain attempt to get her mind off of Tony.

The day dragged. She kept one eye on her phone, the other on the door, expecting to see him barrel in at any second.

Five o'clock came and went. She sent her staff home. She called his cell again, but it was still going straight to voicemail. Finally, in desperation, she called Hannah.

"He's back," Hannah told her calmly, cutting into Julia's questions. "He called me around three o'clock. I thought he was going to call you."

Julia collapsed into her chair. "Why did he call *you?*"

"To ask if we were back."

"He hasn't called me. Why hasn't he called me?"

"I don't know, hon." Hannah's tone was reassuring. "I'm sure you'll see him real soon. I'm guessing he'd rather talk with you in person than over the phone, right?"

"Maybe. Did he sound upset?"

"No. It was strange. He sounded very calm."

Hearing this worried Julia even more. Calm was the total opposite of how she imagined Tony would be feeling. "Okay. Well, I'm glad he's back safe and sound. I guess I'll wait until he comes over."

"I'm sure he'll be over soon."

But he didn't show. Julia managed to keep awake until just after eleven o'clock when she'd finally succumbed to exhaustion and crashed on the couch.

She awoke with a heavy heart and a sense of dread. The first thing she did was check her phone for messages. There were none.

A busy workday loomed. She had three client meetings today and a venue inspection. She was swamped. She'd try reaching him again after work.

At five o'clock, there was still no word.

Julia sat at her desk and stared blankly into space.

She had expected him to come after her. She'd expected him to come hammering on her door, demanding entrance and an explanation. A secret part of her had yearned for that, the heat of a confrontation, the agitation and excitement he aroused inside of her.

But why *should* he come? Hadn't he already proven himself to her?

Was he simply giving her the time and space she'd asked for in the first place? Or, had he given up on her and was already starting the process for an annulment or divorce?

The latter speculation wrenched her heart and filled her with panic.

She was over the fact that he was Joe's brother.

She was over the fact that he was almost six years younger.

He wasn't a rebound guy.

He was the real deal.

She loved him. She loved him more than she'd loved anything or anyone in her life.

She called his cell one last time. No answer. She tried Joe's phone. No answer. She called their company's answering service. The operator informed her that Tony was on a jobsite.

"Do you know where?"

"I don't have an address. It's in Cumberland."

Cumberland. Maybe he was working on his new house.

Their new house.

She was his *wife*.

God, she was such an idiot. She'd been wasting so much time.

She closed up the office and rushed upstairs to take a shower. She shaved her legs and powdered and moisturized her body. Lingerie went flying around the room as she searched for the sexy bra and matching panties she'd purchased on a whim a month before. Then she threw on a pair of jeans and the pink sweatshirt he liked, packed an overnight bag and headed out the door.

Although it was just after six o'clock when she reached Cumberland, it was already dark out and there was a crisp chill in the air; autumn had officially arrived in New England. As she made her way up the drive, her car headlights swept across Tony's truck parked in front of the garage. The front porch light was on, casting a welcoming glow.

Her heart leapt out of her chest when the door suddenly opened and Tony stepped onto the porch. He hesitated for a moment before striding down the front path towards her car. He opened her door.

"Julia."

"Hello."

"What are you doing here?"

She swallowed a couple of times, heart in her throat. She looked up at his stern, forbidding face. Her smile wobbled. "Is that any way to greet your wife?"

He leaned in to push the release on her seatbelt. Then he hauled her out of the car. He latched his hands on her shoulders and held her away from him as he searched her face with narrowed eyes. "Do you *want* to be my wife?"

She lifted her chin. Her smile widened with confidence. "Yes. Always."

"Good." His tone was curt. He removed his hands from her shoulders and jerked his chin towards the front door. "Now get in the house. And get in our bed."

She released a shaky laugh. "Not a man of many words tonight, are you."

He took her arm and spun her around to face the house. He smacked her bottom. Hard. "Go. I'll be right behind you."

In a heady daze, she walked towards the front door. Halfway up the path, she came to an abrupt halt. She pivoted around, finding him inches away. His body heat radiated from him in waves. A muscle ticked in his jaw as he scowled down at her. "Aren't you going to carry me over the threshold?" she asked.

The cold, severe edges of his expression melted away. A warm, fiercely tender light entered his eyes. He slowly shook his head. "Goddammit, Julia Rossetti. You make it impossible for me to stay angry with you."

Without another second of hesitation, he swept her up into his solid arms and strode into the house. He kicked the door shut behind them and then proceeded up the stairs, two steps at a time.

Julia looped her arms around his neck. Possessiveness, hot and sharp, blazed inside of her as her gaze traveled across his features. This man was her husband. "When did you move in?" she asked, her voice trembling with excitement.

"Escrow closed today," he said, not one bit out of breath as he reached the upper landing. "My crew helped me move everything in. In fact, I was just putting the bottom sheet on our bed when I heard you drive up."

She tweaked the comma of soft hair at his nape. "Perfect timing."

He pushed open the door to the master bedroom.

A king-size mahogany sleigh bed stood in the corner.

"Nice bed," Julia said breathlessly.

"Thought you might like it."

He strode towards the bed and tossed her into the center of it. Her body gave a little bounce on landing.

"Ooh, nice mattress. Firm but not too firm. I like it."

"Take off your clothes."

She held his gaze, her blood sizzling at the promise

that burned in eyes, the promise of every deliciously wild and wicked thing she ached for. She shivered. "It's a little chilly in here," she said in a sultry, teasing voice. She eyed the fireplace where a pile of fresh kindling was waiting to be ignited. "Did the previous owners do that?" She nodded at the pre-made fire.

"I did." A corner of his mouth twitched. "Stalling?"

"Not at all. I just remember you saying how much you'd enjoy snuggling with your wife in this room while a fire crackled in the background."

"So I did."

He opened the glass doors to the fireplace, struck a match and set the kindling alight. He waited a few moments until the flames grew stronger. Then he closed the doors and stood up.

He tossed a down comforter on the foot of the bed. "For later," he murmured.

He kicked off his shoes. Then he began to unbutton his shirt. "Hurry up," he ordered. "Get naked."

She tugged off her sweatshirt and tossed it in the corner. "I love it when you get all bossy like that."

One dark eyebrow arched. "Do you? I thought you didn't like it when I get all—what did you call it?—he-man bully."

She toed off her sneakers and rolled off her socks. They followed the same trajectory as the sweatshirt. "I was lying to myself."

He removed his shirt and dropped it to the floor. His eyes lingered on her purple satin and lace bra. "That's a very pretty bra."

She trailed her fingers along the left shoulder strap and down to the demi cup. She touched the place

179

where her nipple was poking against the satin. "Isn't it? I was thinking of you when I put it on."

"Take it off."

"Yes, sir." She reached behind her to undo the fastenings. Slowly, very slowly, she let the bra fall away from her breasts.

He reached for the buttons of his jeans. "I'm only this way with *you*, Julia. I can't help myself. I want to claim you, put my mark on you. You make me wild."

He brushed the knuckles of one hand along the rigid outline of his erection as if to emphasize his declaration.

She followed the motion of his hand with avid interest. Her mouth parted on a breath of anticipation. "You make me wild, too. I've never felt this way before." She lifted her eyes back to his face.

He stepped closer to the bed, the intensity of his gaze making her body sing. "You've always been the good girl, the perfect friend, the perfect daughter. But I've sensed for a long time that there were darker passions burning inside of you."

She threw her bra aside and rose up on her knees. Her gaze returned to his fingers. He'd undone the top two buttons of his jeans. She licked her lower lip. "Come closer. Let me do that."

He moved to the side of the bed until his thighs brushed the edge. He swallowed visibly, and his eyes went half-hooded as she inched closer to him and cupped his crotch.

"Oh, *my*," she murmured.

His startled laugh sank into a groan of pleasure as her knuckles brushed along his naked groin. Julia kept her eyes on his as her fingers undid the rest of the buttons. She watched his eyes widen and the pupils dilate as she tucked her hand inside his briefs and wrapped her palm around the base of his penis.

"*Baby*," he breathed. "You sure?"

"Very sure." She slid her hand slowly, teasingly along his length before bringing both hands to the waistband of his jeans and briefs and tugging them down with unveiled impatience.

He helped her shove his clothing down to his knees. His penis arched up towards his flat stomach, fully aroused, the purplish head glossy.

This was *hers*, Julia thought. All hers. She was going to enjoy playing with it, loving it. A sense of daring and adventure filled her as she thought of all the pleasure she could give him as she mapped the intriguing topography of his body. She slid her hands slowly up his lean torso, fingers sifting through the light matt of hair on his chest. She lowered her head and took him into her mouth.

"Holy...Sweet...*Jesus*," Tony hissed between his teeth as she tasted and nibbled and sucked.

For a while, there wasn't any sound in the room other than his harsh, staccato breaths and gasps of pleasure.

When she cupped his testicles, he brought his hand to her head, fingers tugging at her hair, pulling her away. "As good as this feels, baby, that's all I can take right now. I want to be inside of you when I come."

Julia sat back on her haunches. She wiped her hand across her mouth as she watched him kick off his jeans and remove his socks. When he bent over, the bulbous head of his penis grazed his concave bellybutton.

Feeling desperate to have him inside of her, she

hurriedly unzipped her jeans and flopped onto her back so she could remove them. She felt his hands cover hers as he took over the task. The jeans went flying. Tony dragged her forward to the edge of the bed and placed his hot palm on the crotch of her panties.

"They match your bra," he murmured with appreciation.

She wiggled her hips. "Take them off."

"Oh, I plan to. And I plan to buy you lots of matching bra and panty sets. A different color for every night of the week."

"You mean you don't want me waiting at the door for you each night stark naked? I thought that might be more your style."

His eyes glowed with laughter and desire. "Where's the thrill in that? Undressing you will be half the pleasure."

He trailed a finger slowly along her crotch, outlining her mound, and then pressed down along the center crease. "Feels a little damp under there," he teased.

She arched her hips off the bed. "Take them off and find out just how wet I am for you."

He quickly complied.

He dropped to his knees on the floor, set his hands under her bare bottom and tugged her forward until her bottom rested on the very edge of the bed with her legs dangling. "Spread your legs."

She did.

He tugged gently at the patch of downy blond hair between her legs. "You're so pretty."

She giggled at the masculine appreciation and wonder in his voice. "Thank you."

And then she closed her eyes, her neck arching as he put his mouth on her. His questing tongue laved her soft folds, delved inside her channel, licked its way to her swollen clit. He sucked that tiny bundle of nerves into his mouth at the same time that his hands found and squeezed her breasts.

Julia cried out, canting her hips off the bed as she surrendered to an orgasm that engulfed all of her senses.

When the room stopped spinning, she found herself fully on the bed and Tony above her, his legs between hers, pushing her thighs further apart. He braced his upper body on his hands as he bent his head to take her mouth. It was a soft kiss at first, a kiss of gratitude and promise. Then the kiss caught on fire and burned fierce and hot.

She was out of breath and hungry when he pulled back. He wrapped his big hand over the top of her head, compelling her to meet his piercing eyes. "I want you looking at me when I come into you," he whispered with burning urgency. "I want you saying my name."

She could only nod, too overcome to speak. She brought her hands to his lower back, slid her fingers down to grasp his taut buttocks. She felt the head of his penis touching the crease of her inner thigh. She arched into that hard, hot pressure, sharp currents of need racing up her spine.

"Julia," he breathed as he slowly entered her.

She drew a breath, her mouth agape as he pushed deeper. "Tony," she whispered.

"Louder," he urged. "Say it louder."

"*Tony.*"

His jaw scraped against her cheek. His mouth

brushed her ear. "Who am I?"

"My husband." She undulated her hips, lifting, circling, luring him in deeper and deeper until he was completely inside of her, stretching her, filling her. "Tony."

"Julia," he panted. "My wife."

She slid her arms up his smooth back and clutched his shoulders, pulling herself against him, rubbing her tender breasts against his chest. He lowered himself to his elbows, the tempo of his thrusts increasing. And then he rested his body fully on hers as he slid his hands down to cup her bottom and lift her into his grinding hips.

She loved the sounds he made as he plunged into her—low, soft grunts that were interspersed with shaky sighs that sounded almost like laughter resonating from deep in his chest.

He buried his face against her neck, his breath coming in hot, rapid pants against her skin. He enveloped her completely, filled her completely.

If she could crawl inside of him, she would. She'd never felt this closeness, this total unity. "Tony," she said again as she brought her hands to the back of his head.

She felt the pressure building deep inside of her, her body quickening in preparation for release. She wanted him with her when she reached her peak. "I'm close," she breathed in his ear.

He reared his head back, his eyes seeking hers. At the same time, he snaked his hand between their bodies, his thumb landing unerringly on her swollen clit. He rubbed. "Come with me, baby," he murmured.

Her fingers fisted in the short strands of his hair.

Her mouth fell open on a silent gasp as she convulsed against him and around him. A groan came from low in his chest as he thrust deeply, once, twice and then held still as he released his hot seed deep inside of her. She wrapped her legs around his hips, milking him dry as he bucked through the aftershocks and panted hot gasps against her face.

He brought his arms around her head, cradling her as he collapsed fully against her, his chest rising and falling with the force of his breathing, his sweat-slick skin glued to hers. She was breathing just as hard. She smoothed her hands up and down his back.

A shudder rippled through him and he twitched inside of her. "Julia," he groaned, replete.

"Tony."

She closed her eyes.

He was still inside of her as they both sank into a sated sleep.

Chapter Fifteen

She awoke to feel him flexing slowly inside of her, his penis fully engorged. She opened her eyes to find him braced above her, his hips between her thighs, one hand fisted in the bed sheet, the other lazily playing with her breasts.

"Hello, wife," he said in greeting, his grin cocky.

"Hello." She rocked her hips gently, inviting him deeper.

"Damn. That feels so good. I could live inside of you." He tweaked one nipple with his supple fingers, then brought his head down to suck her other nipple into his mouth.

She sifted her fingers through his hair. "I think a part of you soon will be," she said softly.

He stilled. He released her nipple and lifted his head. His eyes gleamed with love and male pride. "So soon?"

She hitched one shoulder. "I'm not on birth control. And it's the right time in my cycle. And I just have a feeling."

He kissed her mouth tenderly. "Oh, Julia," he whispered against her lips. "That would be a dream come true. Our baby growing inside of you."

He continued to rock slowly inside of her, a

languid coupling as he pressed tender kisses all over her face. Her climax was a gentle ripple, a quiet clenching around his thickness. His orgasm chased hers, his pleasure sounding from deep in his chest.

He rolled onto his back, taking her with him. He caught her close to him, his fingers tracking down her spine and then gently squeezing her bottom. She rested her cheek on his chest, one hand clasped around his neck, her thumb rubbing along his jaw.

Gradually, his penis softened and he slipped out of her. She felt another ripple inside of her, a tiny aftershock.

"Happy?" he asked drowsily.

"Very."

"No more doubts?"

"None."

He glided his hands up her back and massaged her shoulders. "The fire's gone out. Are you cold?"

"Not anymore. Your body is like a furnace."

"How about we try out the Jacuzzi tub?"

"Do you have bubble bath?"

His chest rumbled with soft laughter. "No, I don't have bubble bath stuff. I'm a guy."

"Mmm. Yes you are." She pressed a soft kiss to his sternum. "I *might* have some packed in my overnight bag."

"You brought an overnight bag?"

"Of course. And *maybe* I packed a scented candle, too."

"Any other surprises in there?"

She circled one of his flat nipples. "*Maybe* another pair of panties with a matching bra?"

His penis twitched against her thigh. He groaned.

She grinned. She licked his nipple until it puckered

and then gave it a teasing bite. "You'll have to go get it though. It's still in the car."

He didn't move except to spread his legs, rubbing his burgeoning erection against her. His hands slid down to caress her bottom again. "God, I love your ass."

"I like yours, too."

He chuckled. He slowly eased his penis into her wet channel. "We fit together perfectly, don't we."

She gave a soft gasp as she felt him lengthen and thicken inside of her. "You recover fast."

"Because it's you. Sore?"

"No. Just a nice pleasant ache."

"I'll be gentle."

"Don't be."

As the thrust of his hips picked up speed, she drew herself upright and straddled him, bracing her palms on his hard chest. She felt the thud of his heart vibrating against her right palm.

He cupped her breasts. "You are so beautiful."

"So are you."

"And you're my *wife*." His voice carried amazement.

"Always."

He grasped the back of her neck, drawing her face down to his. His tongue plunged into her mouth, matching the thrust of his hips. She sucked him in, wrapped her hands around his head, pressed her fingers against his skull.

She writhed her hips as he found a pleasure spot deep inside of her. His hot breath mingled with hers. His fingers were between her legs, his thumb rubbing. She was a quivering mass of fever and need. Sweet pleasure pooled and gathered. She tore her mouth from his, cried out in ecstasy as her orgasm surged through her body.

His own cry echoed hers as he spent himself deep inside of her.

They slumbered for a while, her body resting on top of his, exactly where she wanted to be.

Her stomach growled.

He laughed softly. "Hungry?"

"A little."

"Bath first? Or dinner first?"

"What's for dinner?"

"I picked up some roast chicken from the store earlier. How about that with a salad?"

"Sounds lovely."

He gave her bottom a light smack. "Get off of me then."

"No."

He tickled her ribs.

She shot upright, scrambled away from his teasing fingers. "Tony! Stop. I'm ticklish."

"I know."

She vaulted off the bed and raced for the bathroom. She locked the door behind her.

"I'll be downstairs," she heard him call out. "Don't be too long in there."

When she eventually made her way downstairs and into the kitchen, he was putting the final touches on a salad. He had his jeans on and nothing else. His eyes swept over her attire. She was wearing his shirt. It was a cotton work shirt. It draped to mid-thigh on her.

"I like seeing you in my shirt," he said.

She leaned against the center island where he was doing the food prep. "I like being in it."

She admired his washboard abs and the intriguing

line of dark hair that arrowed down to his groin. She reluctantly pulled her eyes away and flicked her gaze around the kitchen. "I like this room."

He scooped large helpings of salad onto two plates. He grinned. "I'll never forget the look on your face the last time we were in this room, when you thought I had a serious girlfriend."

She pursed her mouth. "It wasn't very nice of you to toy with me like that."

"Hey, I was telling the truth. I told you I was thinking of buying this place for my future wife. It wasn't a lie." As he spoke, he sliced up some chicken and put it on another plate. "That was the day I knew for sure that you were attracted to me. Those pretty eyes of yours were practically green with jealousy."

"I wasn't jealous."

"Three days married and you're lying to me already, Mrs. Rossetti?" He winked at her. Then he opened a drawer and withdrew some silverware. He handed it to her. "Here, go set the table. I'll carry everything over."

She strolled over to the small oak table on the far side of the kitchen and set out places for two. "Is this new?"

"Yep. Sylvie wanted the one from the house." He brought their plates to the table. "I haven't brought much furniture from the house. Most of the stuff there is mix and match. I was hoping you'd like to go furniture shopping this weekend."

"Okay. There are a few things at my place that might work here."

He grabbed a bottle of salad dressing from a cupboard and snagged some paper towels. "I like your couch. That might work in the living room. We could get some coordinating pieces." He set the items on the table. "I have water or beer to drink."

"Water's good." She sat down at the table and watched him as he retrieved a pitcher of water from the fridge and then a pair of glasses from a cupboard. "Looks like you already have a lot of things organized. Did your crew help you unpack everything?"

"Just the necessities." He came back to the table, poured their water and then sat down next to her. "There are tons of boxes in the garage. I thought we could go through them together. Decide what goes where."

She scraped her chair closer to his and snuggled against his arm. "You knew I was coming back, didn't you."

"I hoped."

"I thought you were going to come chasing after me," she confessed softly. "I expected you to kick down my door at any minute."

He angled his head to plant a kiss on her temple. "I do have some pride, Julia. I figured there wasn't anything more I could say to you to help you make up your mind. The ball was in your court."

"I'm sorry for being such an idiot."

He lifted her face to his. His eyes were intense. "You are *not* an idiot. You were scared. I get that. You couldn't remember our wedding. I was hoping when you woke up that it would all come back to you. I guess it didn't."

"Were you furious when you realized I'd left?"

"Furious isn't the word for it. I was frantic at first, thinking something bad had happened to you. It was already early evening by the time I woke up. Max was barking like crazy. I had to take him out for a walk. I knocked on Hannah's door on the way because I thought you might have gone there to look at the pictures she'd taken. It wasn't until I called the front desk that I realized you'd both taken off."

"Did you get my message? I called you from Los Angeles."

"Yes. I was in-flight to Chicago when you called. By the time I was able to listen to your message, I was livid. I didn't want to speak to you. It didn't help that I missed the red-eye out of Chicago and spent the night in a flea-bag airport hotel with a yapping dog."

She couldn't help but giggle at the image. She brought her hands to his face and drew him down to kiss his forehead. "I'm sorry."

He kissed her nose. "It'll be a story our grandchildren will want to hear over and over."

She wrinkled her forehead. "So... Where *is* that dog?"

"Max is with Sylvie. I need to get this place dog-proofed before I bring him over. We'll have to make sure to keep the closet doors shut. I've found out that he likes to chew on shoes."

"And just *how* did we acquire that scruffy little mutt?"

His eyes twinkled. "You don't remember?"

She shook her head.

He slid his hands from her face to her shoulders and gave her a nudge. "Let's eat while I tell you all about it."

It turned out that it had been Julia's idea to keep the dog. They were leaving the chapel and Tony was helping her into the taxi when Max had hopped into the car ahead of her and plopped himself down on the seat, tail wagging furiously, a happy grin on his doggy face. He didn't have a collar. His fur was matted and dirty. When Tony had picked him up to remove him from the car, he'd felt the dog's ribs poking out.

"I remember now," Julia said, interrupting Tony's story. "I said there was no way we were going to abandon that poor dog. I insisted we at least take him to the vet to see if he had a microchip."

"He doesn't. And then we had to get him vaccinated so he could travel home with us. After you passed out on me, I gave him a bath." He made a comical face. "That little mutt got to lick your toes. I was lying there thinking 'You lucky bastard. It's *my* wedding day. That's *my* bride'."

Julia laughed. "It felt pretty good, as I recall. You'll have to try it on me sometime."

"Gladly."

She gave him a coy smile. "I thought you wanted a big dog. A lab or a golden retriever."

"Instead I got a mutt of very questionable pedigree." He grimaced. "Who also has cost me close to a thousand bucks already between emergency vet fees, airline fees, hotel fees and all the food he's been guzzling down. He's already put on two pounds since Sunday."

She caressed his arm. "You love him already."

His mouth twitched in a grin. "He has a way about him."

"Consider him my wedding gift to you."

He threw his head back and laughed until his eyes watered. Then he caught her close in a fierce hug. "Oh, Julia. It feels good to laugh about all of this now. These last forty-eight hours have been pretty grim."

"I know." She rubbed her cheek against his warm chest.

He propped his chin on her head. "Do you remember our wedding now?"

"Yes. Most of it. All the important parts." She wrapped her arms around him. "And I'm sorry again for running away, for not believing in you."

"You just didn't believe in yourself." His voice turned gruff. "And I could've been gentler with you that day."

"You know what, though?"

"What?"

"I'm glad that the first time we made love was in this house."

"I would've said differently on Sunday. I was desperate to take you. But I'm glad, too."

She drew back to look him in the eye. "I've been thinking about when to tell my parents about us." She took a deep breath. "I don't think we should tell anyone we're married yet."

His features clouded. "Why not?"

"I want to wait until after Joe and Willa are married," she said reasonably. "I don't want to rain on their parade."

He smiled. "That's very thoughtful of you. It's a good thing, then, that I haven't told Joe about us."

Her relief was tangible. "Oh, good. So only Hannah knows."

"Wait. This doesn't mean you aren't moving in with me until after their wedding, does it? Because I'll be damned if I allow that to happen." His arms tightened around her. "You aren't spending one more night in that apartment."

She snaked her hand between them and gave his chest a soothing pat. "You can come help me pack tomorrow."

He dropped a hand to her bottom and gave it a squeeze. "We'll make it quick. I can't go more than an hour without wanting to touch you. And I'm not going to make love with you in that apartment."

He didn't have to explain the reason why.

She smiled as she felt his questing hand slip beneath the hem of her shirt and wander towards the heat between her legs. "How about we take that bubble bath now?" she suggested, giving a soft gasp as his knuckles rubbed along her damp cleft.

"Are you done eating?"

"I'm not hungry anymore."

"Me neither. Not for food anyway." He wagged his eyebrows and gave her a lecherous smile.

"You are *such* a charmer."

He stood up, taking her with him. "I'll go get your bag out of the car. Why don't you get the water running?"

She hurried upstairs, looking forward to doing naughty things with him in the tub. She was perched on the ledge adjusting the temperature when Tony stepped into the room, her bag in hand. "Here you go. I'm going to get the fire going again."

"Okay."

She poured the vanilla-scented bath soap into the water and stirred it around. While the bubbles formed, she lit the pillar candle she'd tossed in her bag at the last minute. It had a vanilla scent, too.

She'd just turned off the water and was wondering what was taking her husband so long when she heard him call to her from the bedroom.

"Julia, come out here for a minute."

When she walked into the bedroom, the lights were dimmed. Tony stood in front of the fire, the warm glow limning the angles and planes of his chest and face. The intensity of his gaze made her heart flutter wildly. God, he was so handsome. He held out his hand to her.

Curious, excited, she moved towards him, her feet seeming to float. She placed her hand in his palm. He rubbed his thumb across her knuckles. He swallowed. "Julia," he said again, his voice husky.

"Tony."

And suddenly he was dropping to one knee and gazing up at her, both her hands tightly clasped in his.

She felt tears building behind her eyes. Her mouth trembled.

"Julia," he said softly. "I love you. I have always loved you. I *will* always love you. Will you marry me?"

She laughed through her tears. "But we're *already* married."

His kissed her right hand and then her left, his gleaming eyes fastened on hers. "But I didn't ask you formally. And you didn't ask me. It just happened. It was fast. It was beautiful. It was meant to be. But I wanted to do things right. Will you play along with me?"

She had a sudden vision of him as a little boy, throwing pebbles at her window. *Julia. Julia! Will you come outside and play with me?*

She nodded her head. She fell to her knees. "Yes. *Yes*, I will marry you, Tony Rossetti."

He kissed her.

After a while, he whispered against her ear, "I have an idea."

"Hmm?"

"I want you to have your wedding day, Julia. The one you've always dreamed of."

She drew back to stare at him. "It wasn't my dream."

His smile was tender. "Yes, it was. It was your mother's dream, but you wanted it, too." He brushed her face with the back of his hand. "I want us to renew our vows in a church. I want to see you walk down a long aisle on your father's arm. I want our family and friends around us. I want to have a party to celebrate, and I want to dance with you under twinkling lights."

"That *does* sound nice." She knitted her brow. "But I don't want a grand affair, Tony. Seriously. We can have all that but still keep it simple. Can't we?"

"Whatever you want." His cheek dimpled. "Besides, I want to be in your mother's good graces. It's never a good idea to upset the mother-in-law."

She laughed. "She already loves you like a son."

He kissed her again.

"You know what I think?" he said a while later, bemusement in his voice.

"What?"

"I think she and my mom got their signals crossed all those years ago when they both were expecting their firstborn and planning weddings. I think I was already chasing you when I was just a twinkle in my father's eye."

She felt a fresh round of tears forming. "Oh, Tony. What a beautiful thought. I like it. I think you may be right."

"I'm never going to stop chasing you, Julia Rossetti. Around the kitchen. Through the living

room. Up the stairs. Around our bed…"
"And I'll let you catch me every time."
"Promise?
"Always."

Epilogue

He watched her walk down the aisle towards him on her father's arm.

His bride. His wife.

A ray of light beamed from the open door behind her, casting an almost ethereal glow around her. She was an angel, a beautiful vision in white.

He thought of a long ago August day. He'd been searching for sticks at the water's edge while she'd stood on the pier, her back to him, and gazed at the water. She'd been dressed all in white then, too. He remembered being struck by the beauty of her in a deeper way than he ever had been before. He'd paused in his task, tugged his cellphone from his pocket and snapped a picture. He'd had a print made of the picture and tucked it in his wallet. He still had it. He would show it to her tonight when they were snuggled in their bed in front of their cozy fire.

It was New Year's Day. A day of renewal, of fresh beginnings.

His brother stood beside him. Joe and Willa had been married for over two months now. Willa's pregnancy was already beginning to show.

It wouldn't be long now before Julia would look the same. She'd been right; their child had very likely been conceived the first night they'd made love.

Julia's mother sat beside Sylvie in the front pew.

199

Both of them were already crying happy tears.

Across the aisle, Audrey King sent him a big wink.

He winked back.

Julia reached the bottom of the altar. He stepped down to take her hand from her father's.

"Hello, wife."

"Hello, husband."

They shared a secret smile.

"Will you come outside and play with me?" he whispered.

"Yes, I will."

As the congregation of family and friends laughed and clapped, he placed a tender kiss on her lovely mouth.

"Thank you, Julia." he whispered, his eyes reflecting the love beaming from hers. "Thank you for waiting for me."

About the Author

Sophia Renny loves Romance, Chocolate, and Pinot Noir. When she's not writing about strong yet vulnerable men and the women who love them, she can most often be found ignoring housework for the pleasure of engaging in fierce Scrabble competitions with her sweetheart. Yes, she did fall in love with him at first sight. Follow Sophia's blog for updates on future publications, book giveaways, and contests: www.sophiarenny.com

Also by Sophia Renny

Room 1208

Rhode Island Romance Series:

If Ever I Fall (Book 1)

Made in the USA
Charleston, SC
23 June 2015